When the Nightingale Sings

Joan T. Seko

COVER DESIGN BY : EKO SETIAWAN
WWW.FACEBOOK.COM/KYOZESHIROU

"WHEN the NIGHTINGALE SINGS"

Copyright 2020 by Joan T. Seko.

All rights reserved.

All rights reserved. No part of this publication may be reproduced, distributed, or transmitted in any form or by any means, including photocopying, recording, or other electronic or mechanical methods, without the prior written permission of the author, except in the case of brief quotations embodied in critical reviews and certain other noncommercial uses permitted by copyright law.

This book is a work of fiction. Names, characters, places, and incidents are products of the author's imagination or used fictitiously. Any resemblance to actual events or locales or persons, living or dead, is entirely coincidental.

ISBN: 9798664523294

"WHEN the NIGHTINGALE SINGS"

A 15th Century fictional novel during the Feudal period in Japan

The story of the Samurai, Maiko, Geisha, Ronin, and Ninja

The dedication of this book is to five authors who have inspired me to continue my writings:

Kristi Seko Shimada

"Mariko and the Magic Mirror"
"The Enchanted Starflower"

Stella Cameron

New York Times Bestselling Author
of over 80 mystery books

Dee Goto

Omoide books for children

Atsushi Kiuchi

A newspaper reporter and Omoide books

Janine Brodine

"Missing Pieces; Memoirs of World War II"

By JOAN T. SEKO

Book One of Withers' Series: "Lady Dahlia's Story"
Book Two of Withers' Series: "Robin Fish, Spymaster"
"Casha"

PROLOGUE

Masahiro wakes from a sound outside his bedchamber. A roofed corridor, called an engawa, encircles the house, and the hallway makes easy access to the inside. The overhanging roof is a protection against the rain and snow, for the washi-papered shoji doors, and the washi paper comes from the bark of trees. An alarm of a "nightingale singing," will ring through the air, if someone or something unknowingly steps on certain bamboo planks. Masahiro's grandfather installed the alarm when he built the house.

Masahiro knows someone or something is out there, and he throws his quilted futon aside and reaches for his wooden sword. A cat's meow resounds, and Masahiro takes a deep breath and sighs in relief. He hopes his cat, Hanako, is the only presence outside. Masahiro stealthily slides open his shoji door.

CHAPTER 1

Masahiro was born on April 22, 1639. He is fourteen years old, lean and tall, with black hair and brown eyes. Girls glance his way, thinking Masahiro is the most handsome boy in their clan. His grandfather, Mito, and his father, Sange, are samurai warriors. The family belongs to the Ouchi Clan and lives in the Yamaguchi Prefecture of Japan.

The sunlight bathes the cherry trees in full bloom, and the heavy branches bend toward the ground. The fragrance of the spring flowers floats in the light breeze.

In two more years, Masahiro will wear his hair in a topknot—signifying he is a samurai. Masahiro is learning the art of sword fighting during his morning hours. During the afternoon, his tutors teach him to write beautiful calligraphy and poems. Masahiro learns to decipher codes and studies history and mathematics. All clan members receive a good education and learn to have a deep sense of honour. The family pays complete allegiance to their shogun.

It is pouring rain when Masahiro returns to his kendo class. His conical basket hat keeps his clothing and body dry. The Art of Kendo, using a wooden stick, is the prelude to fighting with a sharp steel sword. The teacher often hits him on the top of his head to chastise him. Masahiro cannot yell out in pain—he must gaman—or endure it with a smile.

Both his grandfather and father are renowned throughout Japan, and other clans are in awe of their bravery. Masahiro worries he will not live up to the standards of his ancestors. His grandfather assures him not to worry, and he is very proud of Masahiro's accomplishments.

Masahiro's mother comes from an elite samurai family. Mitsuko is a beautiful woman with black glossy unbound hair that reaches to the floor. The height of her beauty is the length of her hair, and her brown eyes are almond in shape. Mitsuko takes care of all the finances and rules the household with an iron fist. Mitsuko provides excellent care for her parents, in-laws, and children. Her husband is the absolute law, and she humbly obeys.

Mitsuko can handle a sword called a katana and the naginata—a blade on a long staff. These weapons help to defend her home, and if enemy warriors overthrow their estate, she will fight to the end to protect her honour. Mitsuko always carries a small dagger in between her obi sash and silk kimono.

Sange is born one month before Mitsuko. The two families agree on the marriage of their two children when they reach their eighteenth birthday. Love is not a priority—only honour and trust.

Sange watches Mitsuko grow into a beauty. He looks at her from afar, and his heart always beats when she is near. Sange writes sonnets in his journal but is too afraid to send them to Mitsuko. He often wonders what Mitsuko thinks about him. Sange never acknowledges Mitsuko's presence, and she always shyly looks away. There is an attraction between the two.

Mitsuko and Sange celebrate their eighteenth birthday together. The parents turn the party into an engagement celebration. Friends, relatives, and clan members gather to congratulate them. The date of their wedding is June 21, 1638.

Sange goes to a shop in the marketplace to buy Mitsuko, an amulet to keep her safe. The antique shop is over sixty years old, and the shopkeeper, Yutaka, is a young man in his twenties. Yutaka wears his black wavy hair tied back with a navy ribbon, and he has on a navy blue cotton kimono with a blue striped obi. He wears a pair of wooden geta on his feet.

"May I help you pick out something? What is the occasion? I have amulets made of wood, silver, gold, and slips of paper."

"I would like to purchase this miniature gold Buddha to use as an amulet. Tomorrow I will go to the temple and have it blessed, and the omamori will offer my new bride protection from harm. I will ask the priest to write a blessing on a piece of silk fabric and slip it inside. There is a small hole at the bottom, do you have something to seal it?" asks Sange.

"Perhaps you can melt the candle wax. The wax will harden and will make a perfect seal," responds Yutaka.

Sange pays the shopkeeper and heads for the temple. He has the priest bless the Buddha and slip a blessing inside. Sange asks the priest to use melted candle wax to seal the hole. Sange whistles as he happily walks home.

The wedding is an elaborate affair. Mitsuko wears a white brocade silk wedding kimono called shiromuku, and on her head is a wataboshi white hat. Her long black hair is under the white headdress, and her face and neck are painted white, and her lips red.

Mitsuko's teeth are black. The allure of blackened teeth is a traditional sign of beauty. Iron filings have to soak in tea and sake until the iron oxidizes. The water turns black, and the taste is bitter, and flavorful spices rid the liquid of the bitter taste. To do the "okaguro" practice, Mitsuko drinks the dye two or three days before her wedding.

Sange wears his hakama, skirt-like pants over his black kimono, and the hakama is tied at the waist by a unique waistband, and widely flares at the hem. His five-kamon or family crest designs, appear on his kimono on his chest, shoulders, and back. Sange wears a loose outer garment called a haori, similar to a light coat.

The wedding is in two parts. The religious portion is at the Shinto shrine, where the couple marries before a Shinto priest. Only the closest family and a select number of friends attend this ceremony. Daimyo Takayoshi is one of the guests. The daimyo is the head of the Ouchi Clan and answers only to his shogun.

The second part of the wedding is koshi-ire. Maids carry Mitsuko in a basket called a kago to Sange's home. In Sange's garden, Mitsuko and Sange will receive mochi cakes before retiring to their bedchamber.

The bride and groom sip rice wine from three cups and each o-choko is of a different size. They touch their lips to the cups, nine times as a symbolic offering to the God of the Shinto shrine. Mitsuko sips three times from the first o-choko and passes it onto Sange. Mitsuko takes the second cup and does the same. She gives the third o-choko to Sange, and he does not sip but drinks it all. The wedding guests clap their hands in congratulations.

Mitsuko changes her headdress to a hat called tsunokakushi for the reception. The reception is lavish and shows the wealth of both Mitsuko and Sange's families.

Mitsuko says, "I think most brides cry on their wedding day—some in unhappiness and some in joy. Sange, you know mine is in happiness, and don't ever doubt that."

Sange gives Mitsuko the omamori. Mitsuko has tears in eyes as she accepts this wondrous gift from her husband, and Mitsuko grasps Sange's hand and bows in deep respect. Sange laughs and says she is never to bow to him again, and he says she is his equal and not a servant. Mitsuko is now Sange's wife and belongs to the Ouchi Clan.

Two maids are in the garden, lighting white lanterns, and other maids pass out trays of food and drink. Mitsuko beams in happiness now that the ceremony is over. Sange watches his wife and joyously beams.

On Sange and Mitsuko's wedding night, a maid is listening outside the door of their bedchamber. Sange's father needs confirmation that the couple consummates their wedding vows. They want to welcome an heir.

Mitsuko bathes and washes her beautiful long tresses, and her maid, Nori, combs her hair and fans it dry. Mitsuko wears a gorgeous purple silk robe to receive her husband, and Mitsuko lies down on the futon and waits.

Sange is nervous. He is deeply in love with Mitsuko and wants to perform well. Sange withdraws from his bath and puts on a navy silk robe. He slowly walks to their bedchamber, and out of courtesy, he knocks on the shoji door.

"Please come in," whispers a halting voice.

Sange slides open the door, and Mitsuko is lying on top of the quilt. She sits up and asks if Sange would like a cup of rice wine? Sange wants to delay the marriage act, and gratefully accepts Mitsuko's offer.

"*Domo*, thanks," Sange says, reaching for the cup.

Mitsuko lies down and waits. Sange can see Mitsuko's hands trembling, and knows she is petrified of what is going to take place. Sange wants to be gentle. Sange puts down his cup and lies down beside his new bride.

"Mitsuko, don't be afraid. I love you, and I am happy you accepted me as your husband. I pray we will have many children and grow old together. I want to make love to you now. Is that all right?" Sange asks.

When the Nightingale Sings

Mitsuko nods her head and begins to take off her silk robe. She leans toward the lantern on the floor to blow out the candle. Sange shakes his head no. Sange says he desires to see his naked wife in all her glory. Mitsuko's face turns crimson in embarrassment.

Sange says, "Mitsuko, there are no secrets between a husband and wife. We can look at each other's bodies with desire, and there is no reason for any shame between us. I love you, and I hope you will grow to love me too."

Sange begins to caress Mitsuko's body and kisses her neck, and he can feel her shudder as his hands begin to knead her breasts. Mitsuko clutches Sange's neck and draws him close. Sange kisses Mitsuko and places his tongue inside her mouth. Mitsuko's eyes fly open as she looks at her husband in surprise.

Thunder booms and lightning flashes outside their bedchamber. A message from the Gods!

"What is it, Mitsuko? Am I hurting you?"

"No, no. I feel wonderful."

Sange brings his manhood to the entry of her sex. He knows she is a virgin and begins to explain.

"Mitsuko, I am going to hurt you for just a moment, and a wonderful feeling will take its place. Do you trust me?"

"Yes, I trust you, but please hurry—I am in great need."

Sange pushes into Mitsuko, and her eyes look surprised. Sange begins to move, slowly at the beginning, setting a rhythm. He continues to ride her until she cries out in ecstasy, and Sange quickens his strokes until he spills his seeds.

The maid left a large ceramic bowl with a hand towel soaking in lukewarm water. Sange squeezes the water out of the cloth and hands it to Mitsuko to clean herself. Mitsuko turns away, shyly, as she uses the towel.

"Sange, I am bleeding. You must call a physician immediately."

"Mitsuko, it is nothing. I guess your mother never told you about the first time a woman has sex. Remember when you felt that slight pain? That was when I broke your maidenhead. You will have a little bleeding. It is just a natural event, and you are no longer a virgin but a woman."

"My mother did not tell me, and I guess she was too embarrassed. If I have a daughter, I will make certain she knows what occurs on her wedding night. She needs no surprises."

Sange smiles and says, "I would love to have a daughter that looks just like you. I also want sons to carry on my name. We will have to work hard so we will produce many children, and it will be a pleasure to bed you each night. I hope you feel the same."

Mitsuko and Sange fall asleep in each other's arms. It is early dawn when they awaken, and Sange feels a strong urge to make love again. Mitsuko is also ready to engage in their coupling. Sange is so tender in his lovemaking that Mitsuko falls deeply in love with her husband. Ten months later, their son Masahiro is born.

The maid, listening at the door, hurries along the corridor to report to Sange's father—the marriage consummated.

CHAPTER 2

Masahiro's training begins when he is three years old. He is taught how to survive and master the art of kendo. Masahiro learns to wield a wooden pole as a prelude to using a steel sword. The young master will train to use both of his hands when brandishing his sword. As Masahiro grows older, he will prepare for five hours each day. The young master is considered a warrior when he reaches his sixteenth birthday. Masahiro will learn the art of archery and shoot moving targets sitting upon a horse. Masahiro will have to fight a senior samurai or his swordmaster to test his final skills. The young master will learn how to tie up prisoners and to make sure the knot is impregnable. During his rest periods, Masahiro listens and learns from the stories of the older samurai warriors.

Masahiro uses mental discipline to respect his elders and peers.

Mito wants his grandson to try on his suit of armor. The armor is Mito's most prized possession. Masahiro finds it hot and uncomfortable, and it is hard to see out. The armor is protection from their enemy's blades, and if the mask is painted red, it is a sign of anger. The head portion is a painted wooden crest with a nap guard, and there is a shoulder armor, and breast and backplate, fastened together. There is also an armored skirt, hand armor, knee protectors, and a pair of straw sandals to complete the ensemble.

Masahiro's family is wealthy due to their ownership of many acres of rice fields. Whenever they go into battle, they are fighting to gain more land and wealth. The samurai paint their teeth black and tie their hair in a topknot. Their primary weapons are the sword, lance, and bow. The warriors carry two swords, and one is called a katana and the other a wakazashi. The samurai carries a placeholder, made of deerskin, for target practice and a seat to be used for their execution. The samurai live an ascetic life and value courage, bravery, and honour. A samurai usually only lives until forty years of age, and if he lives longer, he is lucky.

CHAPTER 3

Masahiro wakes up early in the morning and eats his breakfast consisting of white steamed rice, miso soup, broiled fish, eggs, and dried seaweed. He sips green tea and pats his full stomach. Masahiro's little brother, Shiso, and his sister, Miho, are still sleeping. His grandfather and father have left on a pilgrimage to Mt. Koya. Masahiro is about to leave for his kendo class when his mother rushes in to say goodbye.

"*Ittekimasu*. I am leaving now."

Masahiro's teacher, Koichi-sensei, is thirty years of age with a muscular body. His hair is tied back with a piece of cloth, and he wears a pair of black pants that balloons out. His cotton top is white and hangs loosely over his pants. Koichi-sensei designed his clothes to make his body more fluid and freer. Sensei is proud he is the only person in the whole of Japan that wears this uniform.

Koichi-sensei is a good friend of Masahiro's father, but he refuses to play favoritism. He is harsher on Masahiro than the rest of the clan's children. This treatment is making Masahiro a worthy candidate for leading the new students.

Masahiro is physically fit and considered tall at five foot seven. Masahiro's temperament is like his mother, his physical dexterity is like his father, and he is fair like his grandfather. Masahiro is an idol to his fellow students.

Masahiro loves to watch the heavens at night and names all the stars. His father taught him how to travel, in the darkness, following the stars above. The only problem with this method is if the heavens are full of rain, snow, or clouds, and fog rolls in—it is impossible to navigate.

Sange teaches his beloved son the martial arts. He hires a ninja warrior to teach his son to be invisible. Masahiro can throw a dagger thirty feet with an accuracy everyone admires. He is nimble of foot, and his intelligence is higher than the average.

Kunio-sensei is a poet, and his gray hair is long and flows haphazardly down to his waist. His brown eyes look like little slits on his chubby face, and Kunio-sensei is overweight and waddles as he walks. The aristocrats of the city revere his poetry. Every day Kunio-sensei asks Masahiro to compose, and Masahiro is becoming an adept poet.

"What masterpiece have you written today?"

"Please accept a small sample of a haiku I have written," bows Masahiro humbly.

The sensei quickly begins to read out loud:

>*"Mirror Moon on Water*
>*Solitary Reflection*
>*Sense of Solitude"*

"This is an excellent start. It emphasizes your sensitive innermost feelings. You may run along now and have a free afternoon."

Masahiro bows to his teacher and happily runs down to a nearby stream. Sakura trees are in bloom, and some of the pink and white cherry blossoms are falling onto the ground. He plucks a low branch of flowers to give to his mother.

The following day after his kendo lessons, Masahiro goes to his history class. Today, Jiro-sensei is explaining the meaning of bushido. Jiro-sensei is wearing a dark brown kimono and a black and brown patterned obi.

"Bushido is the code for Japan's warrior classes. The word bushido comes from the Japanese roots path or way. It simply means a way of the warrior. The principles of the bushido mean courage, honour, and skill in martial arts, frugality, and loyalty to his daimyo above all else. The virtues of bushido include courage, benevolence, righteousness, sincerity, respect, loyalty, honour, and self-control. Bushido is an ethical system and not a religious belief. The ideal samurai is not supposed to fear death. The fear of dishonour and loyalty to his daimyo motivates the true samurai. If a samurai loses his honour, according to the code, he will regain his honour by facing death calmly. The same code goes for his wife and children. The samurai would

have to commit seppuku or what is called a suicide. Seppuku is considered the ultimate in bravery."

Jiro-sensei puts down his long pointing stick and says, "That is enough for today. We will continue tomorrow. You are all dismissed."

Everyone bows and hurries to the mathematics class where Shigeto-sensei is waiting. Shigeto-sensei walks in front of the twenty male students seated on the tatami mats. He is a man around thirty years of age and has a full head of black hair that hangs down to his shoulders. His eyes are dark brown full of alertness. Sensei has on a dark brown kimono with a light brown obi sash. Both he and his students have taken off their hemp sandals and left them in a row outside. Sensei is holding a large sheet of paper with math problems to solve. The students look at the test paper in surprise.

Masahiro takes out his soroban and clicks on the coloured beads. The abacus is easy to operate to perform addition, subtraction, division, and multiplication calculations. The numeric value for each column is shown and updated in the top frame with each bead movement.

Shigeto-sensei asks Shobo, a student, to pass two blank sheets of paper to each student. Shigeto-sensei walks to the teaching board and fastens the test using a hammer and a nail. Masahiro quickly scans the questions to form an answer. There are twenty complicated equations on the board.

Masahiro is in a dilemma. He can't solve the last math problem, and he closes his eyes and tries to form an answer. Masahiro feels a sharp rap on his head, and Sensei is standing next to him with his bamboo stick.

"Have you fallen asleep? I see you still have one problem to calculate. You have five minutes before class is over."

Masahiro snaps to attention as his eyes scan the pages on his test paper. He still cannot answer the last question, so he leaves it blank. In shame, he hands the paper to Shigeto-sensei, bows, and tries to leave the classroom.

"Come back here, Masahiro. Why have you left the last answer, blank? I believe the answer is simple, and you seem not to understand. Return here after all your classes are over. I will help you."

Masahiro cannot believe his teacher wants to help. His sensei always seems to be such a grouch. Masahiro agrees to return in one hour, and he bows as he puts on his sandals.

CHAPTER 4

Masahiro trains for three months, and through kendo, Masahiro gathers self-confidence. He believes the way of the sword is the road to success.

Perspiration runs down Masahiro's back as the August heat beats down and bakes the ground. Masahiro yearns to bathe in the cold waters of the river.

The gleaming wooden floor of the Sei Dojo reflects the morning sunlight radiating into the room through four windows. Masahiro wears a pair of wide navy cotton trousers, a top of the same material, and a quilted vest lined with strips of bamboo. Masahiro wears gloves as a precautionary measure to prevent harm to his hands, and he has on a mesh mask to protect his face. In his hands, he grasps a bamboo sword for practicing. Masahiro and the teacher bow to one another, and Masahiro raises his sword to face-level. Masahiro focuses his eyes on his master, and suddenly, a loud wail comes from Masahiro's throat, as he strikes at the teacher. The sensei counters the attack slashing downwards. In the twinkling of an eye, the sensei disarms Masahiro, and the match is over.

Masahiro walks home after a full day of studying and training. He walks northward along the river as night arrives, and he looks up at the light of the moon and hears a sound. The noise comes closer, and Masahiro comes to a halt. He begins to laugh as he sees the two sparkling yellow eyes of his cat.

"Hanako, did you come to welcome me home?"

"Meow!"

Masahiro snaps off a leaf from the bamboo bush near the gate of his home, and he sticks it into his mouth and begins to suck. He removes his sandals and enters. Inside he finds his mother sitting on the tatami floor, arranging a peony into a beautiful ceramic vase. Masahiro's mother places a sprig of pine alongside the single white flower.

While making an ikebana composition, Mitsuko needs total silence. It is a spiritual experience that helps her develop closeness with nature to merge the indoors and outdoors. Ikebana is not just about putting a flower into a container; it is about the devotion to create a beautiful display. Ikebana is about, Mitsuko, who is arranging it.

In the middle of the wall is a shelf where his mother will eventually place the arrangement. On the alcove wall, hangs a scroll with Chinese calligraphy in black ink. The shoji door, to the left, is open to a marvelous view of their Japanese garden. Within the confines of the garden is a pond filled with multicoloured koi. The carp are beautiful, showing colours of red, gold, orange and black.

"*Tadaima, Okasama.* I am home, Mother."

"*Okairinasai.* Welcome home, Masahiro."

Mitsuko leads Masahiro into the garden. Within reach, there is a tray with a teapot, a small lacquered box, and two teacups. She claps her hands, and a young maid brings in hot water and fills the teapot. Mitsuko uses a small lacquered spoon to scoop powdered tea into the two cups, and she adds the hot water. She uses a bamboo whisk to stir the powder until it foams. The maid places a dish of sweet bean cakes in front of Masahiro, and Mitsuko urges her son to eat and drink.

"*Itadakimasu*! Thank you for the food."

Masahiro rolls his eyes in contentment. The bean cakes are delicious. His mother smiles as she hands him an oshibori, a small wet towel to use as a napkin.

"Dinner will be ready in one hour. If you wish, you may first take a bath?"

Masahiro decides to take a bath and change his sweaty clothes. He sets his new clothes and towel on top of a wooden shelf and quickly undresses. He scrubs his body from head to toe and uses a wooden pail filled with warm water to douse the soap from his body. Masahiro climbs into the ofuro and soaks.

CHAPTER 5

Mito and Sange are on their way to Mt Koyasan in the remote wooded area of Wakayama Prefecture. Sometimes people call it Mt. Koya, and it is the headquarters of the Shingon School of Buddhism. It is a sacred spot, and Masahiro's grandfather and father make yearly pilgrimages. Mito and Sange are riding horses, and their saddlebags hold extra clothes, food, and supplies.

Mito and Sange carry two lunch boxes for their journey. Inside both obento boxes are three rice balls stuffed with umeboshi, a salted plum paste, and each onigiri wrapped with a thin piece of dried seaweed. Several slices of egg rolls and a handful of sweetened black beans are also inside. Each man carries a flagon of water.

When the Nightingale Sings

Sange and Mito sit on a log near a bubbling brook. They unwrap their lunch and begin to eat with delight. The horses are chomping at the grass and drinking water. It is already five hours since leaving home, and Mt. Koya is a few more miles down the road.

Sange stretches and goes to the stream to wash his hands. As he bends over, he sees a flash of steel as the knife whizzes past his head. He shouts out a warning to Mito, and they both hide behind a large boulder. Mito and Sange watch as a man leaps down from a tree dressed in all black and wearing a mask over his face.

Mito calls out, "Who are you, and what do you want?"

The man roars with laughter and says, "I have come to chop off your heads."

Mito shouts, "Who has sent you? We do not intend to die this day, and you best be on your way if you value your life. My son and I are samurai warriors from the Ouchi Clan, and will fight you to the end."

The man reaches for his weapon, and Sange and Mito step out from behind the boulder, unsheathing their swords. Mito and Sange circle the intruder and try to strike him, but the man is quick, and steps quickly out of reach. Mito and Sange force the man to the edge of the river, and Mito strikes forward, and the man topples into the rapids. Sange and Mito watch in horror, as the man is battered against the rocks as he speeds downriver. They wonder who sent him.

Mito and Sange feel uneasy as they gather up their things. Instead of going to Mt. Koya, they decide to return to their estate. They reach home in the evening and find everything is normal. Mitsuko greets her husband and father-in-law in surprise.

"What has happened? Why are you back? Are you feeling poorly? Come into the house and let me get you some tea."

Mito asks, "Mitsuko, has anything strange taken place since we left? A stranger accosted us, and he fell into the river and battered on the rocks. I think he is dead, but I can't be sure. I need to find out who sent him and why he wants to hurt our family. Tomorrow I will visit Daimyo Takayoshi and ask for his assistance. Tonight I will post guards to watch over our estate."

Mitsuko gathers the servants and tells them to report anything out of the ordinary. She warns, someone may try to enter the estate, and guards already posted.

Sange rises, trying not to wake his wife and goes to check with the posted guards. Sange steps onto the roof and raises a blue flag to alert the Ouchi Clan of imminent danger. He sends messengers to the members of the clan in warning, and everything remains peaceful through the night. Sange knows his enemy is cunning and may suddenly appear. Tomorrow Sange will visit his daimyo and ask for aid. Sange returns to his bedchamber and falls asleep.

Masahiro wakes from the sound of the alarm outside his shoji door. The bamboo planks are singing the "nightingale song." He slowly rises from his bed, grabs his kendo stick, and silently approaches the door. Masahiro raises the kendo pole high above his head and opens the door. The cat leaps into the room and rubs herself around Masahiro's legs. Masahiro peers out into the darkness and is relieved it is only his cat.

"Hanako, you almost gave me a heart attack."

"Meow!"

Weeks go by, and no new attacks come. Daimyo Takayoshi assures Mito that it was a random rogue that wished them harm. A month later, Mito leaves two guards—one at the front gate and one at the back of the house.

CHAPTER 6

Traditional Japan embraces sexual delights, and men are unfaithful to their wives when the men visit a courtesan. Love is not essential in an arranged marriage. The main job of a wife is to manage the home and produce heirs. For sexual gratification, the men go to the courtesans that live in walled-in pleasure houses known as yūkaku.

Sange takes Masahiro to visit a house of ill repute, and it is a rainy night in May of 1655 when they enter the pleasure palace. A pretty young courtesan in a bright coloured kimono greets them. Paperwhite lanterns are hanging from the ceiling, casting shadows against the bedchamber walls. Sange removes a small cloth bag from his kimono sleeve and hands a payment to the young girl. She bows and accepts the coins, and Masahiro watches his father exit the shoji door.

Masahiro is terrified and has no idea what to do. He looks at the young girl that is removing pins from her hair, and her black silken tresses flow down her back.

"My name is Ritsuko. Come here and sit by me, and don't worry, I will not hurt you. Is this your first time? What is your name?"

"My name is Masahiro, and yes, this is my first time visiting this place. I have no idea what I am doing here, and I didn't think my father would just leave me without explaining the situation. I think I need to leave, would you please call me a rickshaw?"

Ritsuko giggles into her hands. She looks up at Masahiro and says, "You need not be frightened, I will take care of you and teach you the art of making love. That is the reason your father left you here."

Masahiro is startled! He can't believe his father left him so he can learn the art of love. What type of discipline is this? Masahiro sits in disbelief and wonders what is in store for him.

Ritsuko begins to take off Masahiro's kimono. She takes off his tabi socks and tickles his feet. Masahiro can feel his toes curling as the sensation runs up his legs. Before, long he is down to his underwear. He looks down, and his face turns crimson.

The courtesan calls for the maid, and Masahiro quickly covers himself with his kimono. The maid appears with a large bottle of sake and two cups, and Ritsuko pours the wine and hands a sake cup to the young master. Masahiro grabs the o-choko and quickly drains it with one gulp. The courtesan is astonished and tells Masahiro to slow down, or he will get drunk. Masahiro doesn't care—he is too nervous and embarrassed.

The maid leaves, and Ritsuko begins to undress. Off comes her obi—off comes her kimono—off comes her undergarments—off comes her tabi socks. Masahiro shyly glances away. Masahiro has a younger sister, but he has never seen her unclothed.

Ritsuko tells Masahiro to lie down on the cushioned bed on the floor. Masahiro wants to leave, but now his curiosity is getting the best of him. Masahiro is feeling a strange awakening that he has never felt before. His manhood is suddenly becoming hot and stiff. Masahiro tries to cover his dilemma with his hands.

Masahiro turns away as Ritsuko lies next to him. She begins to stroke Masahiro's body, and she kisses him. He moans, and suddenly a spurt of white sticky liquid sprays across his stomach. Masahiro feels a welcome release, and his eyes close.

Ritsuko laughs and says, "Masahiro, you are too quick. You need to satisfy your mate as well as yourself. Now, we will try again."

Hours into the morning, the seduction continues, and Masahiro is in ecstasy. The visit to the courtesan is the best gift his father has ever bestowed. Masahiro is tired, but he still wants more, and Ritsuko gives him more.

Masahiro sleeps like a rock, and when he wakes, Ritsuko is gone. Masahiro dresses and goes in search of her.

"Can you tell me where Ritsuko is? I would like to thank her for a wonderful evening."

The young maid answers, "She is gone. Ritsuko will return in three days. You can come back at that time."

"*Domo arigato gozaimasu.* Thank you very much. Please tell Ritsuko I will come back in three days."

Masahiro steps out of the pleasure palace gates and finds his father waiting. Masahiro is embarrassed to look into his father's face. Masahiro's father pats the back of his son's shoulders and laughs in merriment.

"Did you have a pleasant night? I hope you did. I was just sixteen when your grandfather brought me to this pleasure palace. Of course, the courtesans have changed; otherwise, they would be old enough to be your mother."

Masahiro hurries after his father to the rickshaw. His initiation to the world of sex is over, but he relishes the memories. Masahiro wonders if his mother knows where he spent the night. Did she give permission?

Sange calls for Masahiro the following Saturday, and he is going to take Masahiro to the Nishimori Teahouse. Masahiro thinks it is another pleasure palace, and grins, as he follows his father to the rickshaw.

The rickshaw stops in front of a large house with many steps to climb to the front entrance. There is a guard monitoring who can pass through the front door. To Masahiro's surprise, the guard waves them through the entry, without asking their names.

A maid greets Sange and Masahiro and takes them into a large tatami room. There is a beautiful geisha dressed in a silk kimono sitting on a cushion. She is in a muted green silk kimono with gold interwoven threads, and her obi is green with black and gold stripes. Akiminiko's hair sweeps upwards, and her face is painted white. Akiminiko's hairstyle is of a young geisha and called momoware, and means split peach. The geisha has a small ornament in her hair and a red rouge on her bottom lip. On her feet, she wears white socks called tabi, which buttons along the side with a tight fit. Akiminiko bows as Sange and Masahiro enter.

"Lord Sange, it is a pleasure to have you here. I understand you have brought your son to enjoy the evening."

"Hai, yes, this is my son Masahiro. He is sixteen. I have brought him so you can teach him about the world of the maiko and geisha, and I will remain here with him this evening. Please serve us some sake."

Akiminiko calls out, and a maid appears with a bottle of sake. Akiminiko's long elegant hands pour the rice wine into two delicate sake cups. Another maid appears with food. There are thin slivers of raw fish called sashimi, elegantly sitting upon a crystal dish. The maid hands Sange and Masahiro hot wet towels, called oshibori, to wipe their hands.

A young girl around the age of seventeen is sitting in the corner of the room. She has on a colourful bright-pink kimono. Seto is a maiko and is quietly observing Akiminiko's entertainment techniques.

An older geisha enters the room. She is wearing a beautiful dark blue silk kimono. The patterns on the kimono are of two peacocks at the bottom near the hemline. The older geisha sits down behind a stringed instrument called a koto, and begins to strum. Akiminiko stands and begins to dance. The odori is mesmerizing, and Masahiro's mouth gapes open.

Masahiro wears an expression of astonishment and seems to sense the very essence of the dance. The music is melodic as the older geisha sings a bitter song of her lost love—Akiminiko dances like a woman robbed of life and happiness. At the end of the dance, Masahiro has tears in his eyes, and he brushes them away before his father can see the emotion he is displaying.

The koto is a long Japanese board zither having thirteen silk strings and movable bridges. The body is made of paulownia wood and is seventy-four inches long. The older geisha begins to sing another song in accompaniment to the instrument she is playing. Akiminiko takes out a fan, from her bosom, and opens and closes it as she turns.

Akiminiko's day starts long before Sange and Masahiro's appearance. She rises at five in the morning and eats her breakfast. At the hairdresser, she bends over a sink, and a warm container of water poured over her head. The hairdresser applies soap and proceeds to scrub Akiminiko's hair in painful strokes. Next, the hairdresser combs her hair with oil to make it shine. Soft wax is combed through Akiminiko's hair until evenly distributed. The hairdresser brings the forelock back, and the rest of her hair comes up into a knot, looking like a pincushion. The appearance of Akiminiko's hair, from the rear, seems as though split in two. The split peach effect is very erotic, and men find it to signify a woman's body part.

Seto's day begins almost like Akiminiko's. It takes Seto two hours to put on her makeup and clothes. Seto's kimono type is seasonal. In spring and autumn, she will wear a lined and thinner kimono called Ro and Sha—worn in summer. In winter, the kimono is a warm double-lined dress called nemai-awase. Besides, the kimono creates a sense of season, such as choosing one like seasonal flowers as patterns. Seto's kimono is tailored to have a longer hem and can weight as high as forty pounds. When Seto walks outside, she will walk with her left hand holding the heel (between the belt and the hem). If it is raining or snowing, Seto can lift the hem of her kimono.

Seto will choose an obi according to the month of the year in a fixed floral motif. In January, the obi might be in pine, bamboo, plum blossom, rice ear, turtle and crane, string ball, or chrysanthemum—in February, plum blossom or pinata ball. Canola flowers, narcissus, peach or peony in March—in April, she may wear cherry blossoms or Goro butterfly—in May, wisteria or iris—in June, hydrangea or willow—in July, Gion paper fans, fireworks, or goldfish. The August motif is Japanese pampas grass or morning glory and in September bellflower, Japanese clover, or yellow patrinia. October will only be the chrysanthemum and November, either maple or ginkgo. December will be more festive with New Year decorations called "mochibana," or "takeyara" (bamboo craft).

Akiminiko puts on her tabi and proceeds to pick out a subtle blue kimono in a gold floral design at the hemline. The white-collar of her kimono arch down in the back, and it is so low, you can see the first few bumps of her spine. The neck of a geisha is sexy.

Akiminiko's obi is called a "maru-obi, and Seto's obi is called a "dangling obi." The heavy bright floral brocade is knotted almost to Seto's shoulders and comes cascading downwards to her ankles. Seto's obi is so heavy she cannot tie it herself, and a man called an otokoshi helps her complete her wardrobe. At the end of the obi is the crest of the okiya to show which house Seto belongs. Seto's collar is red while she is a maiko, and when she becomes a geisha, she will have a "collar change" or "Eri-kae."

Akiminiko wears a pair of geta on her feet. Seto wears high; unpainted wooden clogs called an okubo.

Putting on makeup is one of the finishing touches. Akiminiko uses a flat brush in a dish of water to make a chalky white paste. She uses the white paste to paint her face and neck. Akiminiko leaves her eyes bare as well as around her lips and nose. She takes a smaller brush and dampens it to fill in around the nose and eyes. Akiminiko tints her cheeks a light pink and her bottom lip a bright red. The upper lip is left white to make the bottom lip look fuller. Akiminiko fills in her eyebrows with a piece of charcoal. Silk flowers and ornaments are on Akiminiko's headdress. A touch of perfume is on the back of her neck, and a small vial of perfume hides in Akiminiko's obi. Akiminiko places a folded fan into her obi and stows a handkerchief inside her kimono sleeve.

The maiko must master the four steps of putting on makeup:

1. Apply "Bintsuke" wax on face, neck, and back as a base.
2. Dissolve kneaded white paste in water and apply it using a broad flat brush.
3. Draw eye lines and eyebrows with a black and red stick called "bo-beni."
4. Apply the red on the lips. Maiko, in their first year, typically apply the beni to only the lower lip.

When applying white on the neckline, Seto will make a linear pattern. This pattern is called a "leg" or "ashi." and it is a trick to make the neck look long and beautiful. The maiko will usually have "two legs" when visiting a regular banquet, and "three legs" for more formal settings.

Akiminiko's thoughts begin to stray as she recalls the "mizuage ceremony." It was a bidding war to deflower her as a virgin when she was fifteen. The men's bids for Akiminiko were the highest ever recorded in her geisha house, and her okiya prospered. Konoye oka-san, the owner of the geisha house, was able to pay off all Akiminiko's debts.

On Akiminiko's fifteenth birthday, Konoye oka-san, calls Akiminiko to her bedchamber.

"Akiminiko, it is time for you to become a woman. I have made arrangements for your "mizuage ceremony." It will take place in two weeks, and I will prepare you for what is to come. Invitations are going to high-ranking officials, samurai clans, and wealthy businessmen. The men will bid against one another to earn the favor to make you a woman. The highest bidder will take your virginity, and I cannot release his name, without his permission. You may never know who helped with your awakening. The highest bidder will join you in a special darken bedchamber that I will prepare in advance. You will take a hot bath and eat a light supper. A maid will help prepare you for your awakening."

Akiminiko becomes fearful, and her throat is dry, and tears are streaming down her cheeks. Her kimono feels damp from her perspiration, and she feels her heart rapidly beating. The last time she had this same feeling was when her father sold her to the okiya. The other geisha in the house tells Akiminiko about their ceremony, and Akiminiko is more and more in distress.

On the day of the "mizuage," or what is known as "raising the waters," a maid brings Akiminiko into the special bedchamber and places two futons on the tatami floor. The maid hands Akiminiko a small vial of oil and tells Akiminiko to place a minuscule drop onto her genitals. The maid promises it will help to complete the sex act.

The maid picks up the bedchamber lantern and moves it to a corner of the room. The room is now dark, and Akiminiko can only see shadows.

Akiminiko can hear the maid greet the highest bidder, as he enters the bedchamber.

The winning bidder asks Akiminiko to lie down. He slowly begins to undress her. He tells her to put a towel underneath her hips to soak up any blood and fluids that may flow. He begins to explain the process of breaking through her maidenhead.

"For women, it is always painful to perform sexual intercourse for the first time. I will have to break through a barrier to reach fulfillment. There will be some bleeding, but nothing alarming. It is my honour to be your first lover, and I will cherish your sacrifice for the remainder of my life."

Akiminiko closes her eyes and can feel the man's fingers on her breasts as he pinches and fondles. The patron moves Akiminiko's legs apart, kneels, and settles between them. There is hardly any foreplay, and his body is above her as he lowers himself. The patron begins to push harder, as the lubricant Akiminiko has administered, helps push him inward. He begins to move, and she feels a sharp pain! She can hear the patron's heavy panting just before he releases a low moan. For a few moments, the patron does not move, and Akiminiko can feel the heaviness of his body as she struggles to be free. The patron rises and rushes to the bathhouse.

A maid enters and hands Akiminiko, a small packet wrapped in paper and tied with a piece of string. Inside are Chinese herbs to deter pregnancy. She is happy her awakening was a success, and she will never have to go through it again.

Suddenly, Akiminiko comes back to the present. Sange is speaking to her.

"Pour me another cup of sake, and pour one for my son too. We are leaving in a few minutes, and Masahiro will come back here next week. Please take care of him"

Akiminiko nods as she smiles at Lord Sange and Masahiro. She goes to the sliding door to let her two guests depart. She steps into her geta and leads Sange and Masahiro to a waiting rickshaw. The wooden shoe has lacquered thongs to hold her feet in place.

The young geisha bows, as Lord Sange and Masahiro, step into their rickshaw. She lowers her head in respect until the rickshaw is out of sight.

Akiminiko removes her makeup, strips off her clothes, and readies herself for a bath. After her bath, she wears a yukata, a cotton kimono nightwear, and ties it with a small obi. Akiminiko opens a jar of white cream and begins to lather it over her skin. The young geisha cannot use an ordinary pillow to sleep and takes out a takamakura, a cradle for the base of her neck. The padding is a bag of wheat husk. Akiminiko's hair is suspended in the air, keeping her hairdo from ruin. She quickly falls asleep.

There are many lessons that Akiminiko has to learn. Her teacher is strict and reprimands Akiminiko's performance if below standard. She excels in playing the flute and drums but has difficulty playing the shamisen. The shamisen is a lute instrument using three strings, and it has a long neck and is thirty inches long. Its body is made of wood and covered with cat or dog skin.

Akiminiko begins to sing. Some girls cannot carry a tune, but fortunately, Akiminiko has a sweet soprano voice that is soft and pleasing to the ear. All the geisha must first learn to sing before becoming good classical dancers. A singer playing the shamisen always accompanies the dancers.

Dancing is one of the most important things that a geisha performs. Akiminiko knows how to dance to pure perfection, and she is attractive and talented. The geisha keeps a stoic expression like the Noh masks they sometimes wear. If there is a misstep, the okiya mother will use her closed fan to strike the side of her head or hand. Akiminiko strives to be not only a good dancer but a great one!

Akiminiko must master the proper etiquette of a refined woman. She cannot slouch or walk-in long strides, and Akiminiko's toes must always point inwards. Akiminiko's body parts, such as her fingernails and toenails, are kept clean and neat. She is required to speak intelligently with warmth. Akiminiko has to remind herself she is an entertainer and has to learn the art of keeping a man well-entertained. Akiminiko knows she is not a maid and does not have to be at the beck and call of a man's needs.

Tea Ceremony lessons are a must, and the tea itself is from ground-powdered tealeaves. Akiminiko combines the powdered tea and tepid water by using a bamboo whisk, making a frothy green tea called matcha. The taste is bitter, and something sweet always accompanies the matcha to set off the bitterness. Most parties at private homes begin with the serving of green tea. Akiminiko finds the tea ceremony is calming, in comparison to her frazzled music lessons.

Akiminiko has music lessons in the mornings, works in the afternoons and evenings, and only sleeps three to five hours each night. Akiminiko is a favorite hostess, and requests for her company are numerous.

Konoye oka-san tells Akiminiko that the first geisha were men called taikomochi or houkan, and the taikomochi were attendants to the daimyo. Male geisha originated in the 1200s from the 'J, sect of Pure Land Buddhism. The houkan were the sounding boards for military strategies, and the men battled at the side of their lord. The male geisha advised and entertained their lord and came to be known as doboshu or comrades. The comrades were tea ceremony connoisseurs and artists. Later they were known as otogishu or nanashishu that translated to storytellers.

Akiminiko is a proper high-class geisha. The lower-class geisha women are sometimes available for sexual favors. Any man who desires Akiminiko cannot purchase her for a night-filled with sex. She is a geisha of the first tier.

The goal of a Geisha is to find a danna or a man as a patron. A wife for her husband usually uses this term. A geisha that refers to her danna isn't speaking of her husband. The geisha never marries. If a man desires a long time relationship with a geisha, and she finds him pleasing, they may end up in a long-term arrangement. The man will pay the okiya, or what is known as a geisha house, to cover her living expenses, meals, gifts of jewelry, kimono, lessons, spending money, and an hourly fee when he meets with her.

Akiminiko is looking for a special man to be her danna. She is still young, but Akiminiko can't wait much longer. She dreams about finding a dashing young patron that will turn her head.

Akiminiko is eleven years old when her father sells her the geisha house, and Akiye is the oldest of six children. Her father is a farmer with a small plot of land that is not sufficient enough to feed his large family. Akiye is crying as she hangs onto her mother's kimono. Akiye's name is changed to Akiminiko when she is adopted.

At the age of twelve, Akiminiko begins to look womanly and is quite tall. Men take notice of her as she walks down the street. Akiminiko doesn't know what to make of the attention she is drawing from the opposite sex. She listens to them whisper and says; she is the most beautiful girl they have ever seen.

One day, a man appears at the okiya. He has silver tinged hair and is around forty years old. His silky navy kimono and blue obi sash are elegant. He is distinguished and quite handsome for his age. The man has asked to meet Akiminiko because he wants to give her a gift. Konoye oka-san has reminded the man that Akiminiko is still too young to form a relationship.

The man is seated in the visitor's reception room, waiting for Akiminiko, and patiently sipping tea. Akiminiko raps on the shoji door, to announce her arrival, and slides open the door. She doesn't recognize the man and bows. He tells her to enter, and sit opposite him, as he points to a red floral patterned cushion. He hands her a bundle wrapped in a purple silk striped furoshiki and tells her to open the gift and watches as she unties the fabric. Akiminiko gasps as she sees a magnificent silk kimono. She looks at the man questioningly. The man rises and says he is only the messenger and leaves.

Akiminiko is in shock as the man disappears, and she rushes out to the road to search for him. Akiminiko looks down the roadway and watches a palanquin going around the corner. Akiminiko runs back inside in search of Konoye oka-san. Unfortunately, Konoye oka-san does not know the man's identity.

Akiminiko realizes she is still a teenager, but in a few years—a grown woman. She never hears from the man again, and she waits for the man of her dreams.

Konoye oka-san is teaching Akiminiko the art of proper bowing. She tells Akiminiko to sit further away from the low lacquer table to make room.

"Now sit up tall with your knees bent beneath you. Spread your hands onto the tatami mat and lean forward—bow as low as possible and keep your neck straight. Don't drop your head, and don't put pressure onto your hands. That's not bad—just keep practicing. Now, let's try it again."

Akiminiko starts as a Maiko, and the term translates into a child dancer. Although women of twenty-one to twenty-three can train to be a geisha without becoming a maiko, having been a maiko first ups Akiminiko's worth and prestige.

The okiya mistress spends a great deal of money training a new apprentice. The protégé is in debt from the moment she enters. Konoye oka-san is a strict taskmaster, but she is happy that Akiminiko is an apt student. Konoye oka-san knows this new beauty brings her house much fame and fortune.

One autumn day, a man comes calling and asks for Akiminiko. The mistress says Akiminiko is out and will be back in two hours. The man says he would like to wait and asks for a cup of tea. Konoye oka-san leads him to a small tatami room and has the maid bring him the beverage.

Three hours pass, and Akiminiko arrives home. Konoye oka-san tells her she has a visitor. When Akiminiko knocks on the door, there is no answer. She slides open the door and finds the man fast asleep on the floor. Akiminiko gently nudges his shoulder, and his eyes fly open. Akiminiko gasps as she looks into the man's face. He is a carbon copy of the gentleman Akiminiko received the beautiful kimono from when she was thirteen. This man is handsome and much younger.

"I am Akiminiko. Did you wish to see me?"

"Yes, my name is Tsutomu, and I am a samurai from Sendai. My father visited you many years ago and gave you a kimono. Do you remember him?"

"Of course I do. The kimono is my prized possession. I am saving it for an auspicious day before I wear it. Thank your father for me."

"My father peacefully died this last winter from tuberculosis. He was a wonderful man and a loving father, and I miss him every day. The reason I am here is that when you were still a young girl, I saw you from the street. You were coming out of the okiya, and I fell deeply in love with you at first sight. I made my father buy you that kimono and made him give it to you as a gift. I know you are a geisha now, and cannot leave this okiya, and will spend the rest of your life as a single person. If I cannot persuade you to come to live with me as my wife, I can only ask if I can be your sponsor?"

Akiminiko is stunned. She trembles as she looks into Tsutomu's sincere eyes. She feels so happy to have such a wonderful man as her danna.

"Yes, it would be my honour to have you as my danna. I cannot say I will not wed you someday, but at this moment, I cannot. I have vows taken as a courtesan, and I must be true to my word."

Tsutomu sighs in relief.

"I will go tell Konoye oka-san, I am now your danna. Please wait here until I return."

Akiminiko can't believe her luck as she changes into the beautiful kimono. Akiminiko's old life ends, and a new life begins.

Tsutomu remains Akiminiko's danna through the years. He pays for all her debts and gives her kimonos and jewelry. Tsutomu waits, patiently, for Akiminiko to leave the okiya to become his bride.

CHAPTER 7

Mitsuko is in the market. Two maids are helping her carry fresh vegetables, meat, and fish. Usually, Mitsuko does not go shopping, but today Daimyo Takayoshi and his aide are coming for dinner, and this is a great honour, and she wants to make the meal the envy of the other clan member's wives. There will be a total of twenty guests.

The maids are scurrying as they set the tables. There will be one short table in the middle with two long tables on each side. The short table will seat Daimyo Takayoshi and his aide Kazu—Mito, and Lord Sange as their hosts.

"Nori, where is the hashitate—the chopstick holders? We need to use the black lacquered chopsticks with the Ouchi crest. Make certain the kamon is visible and not upside down. Bring the sake cups and place them at each place. Hurry, we don't have much time," orders Mitsuko.

Nori sets the chopsticks onto the table and rushes to the kitchen. Mako, the chef, is in distress. Mako is ranting and raving as he waves his arms.

"Where is the kazunoko? I need to marinate the fish roe at once. Did you forget to buy it? Someone must go back to the market at once."

Tamiko looks under a large package of leafy vegetables and finds the roe. The maid triumphantly waves it above her head. Mako glares at Tamiko while he slices the sashimi. The shrimp is still alive, and it is squealing and moving its tentacles. The sea bream is twitching, and the slices look like moving waves. Mako shakes his head in delight, knowing how fresh the seafood will appear to the guests. Nori grates the wasabi and sets it upon a small plate. The horseradish is green in colour and spicy. Several containers of soy sauce are on the tables.

Sange hires a geisha to entertain. Sange asks for Akiminiko, but Akiminiko is at another engagement. Konoye oka-san, the mother of the geisha house, assures Sange, Maki is a wonderful hostess.

Maki arrives at the appointed hour of seven. She wears an aquamarine kimono with designs of ocean waves, and Maki's obi is a deep orange with flecks of silver and gold threads. Maki's hair is swept up and adorned with an ornamental hairpin called a kanzashi.

Sange hurries down the corridor to meet Maki. The Geisha is carrying her shamisen wrapped in a silk fabric, and Sange summons a maid to show her to a dressing room to prepare.

The male guests arrive one by one, and Daimyo Takayoshi walks in with his aide, Kazu. The members of the Ouchi Clan rise and bows to their leader. They sit cross-legged before the low lacquer table.

The men wear a two-piece costume called the hitatare style. Daimyo Takayoshi's kamon is on the sleeves of the samurai warriors, and they wear it with pride for this auspicious dinner.

All weapons of the samurai guests are in a small room by the entry. The samurai of the Ouchi Clan are always relieved of their weapons to instill peace while eating and drinking. A posted guard stands in front of the storage room to ensure no harm will come to any of the guest's weapons.

The samurai swords go through an obi belt worn wrapped around the waist and tied in front. The men also carry a short sword named a wakizashi or a knife called a tanto. The swords are always worn on the left side even if the men are left-handed.

The traditional hairstyle of the samurai is the topknot, and the kimono is the primary everyday clothing. The warriors' clothes are silk; the quality of the fabric depends on the samurai station in life. The older samurai tend towards shades of gray or brown kimonos, in keeping with their age.

Beneath the kimono is a fundoshi of two different varieties. One fundoshi looks like a diaper, and the other underwear is a long loop that is slung around the neck fastened to the top of the loincloth, while the other end is pulled up around the other side of the stomach, and tied around the front of the lower waist with cords.

The samurai has the option of wearing tabi socks that has space to separate the big toe from the other toes. This separation enables the warriors to wear sandals. The samurai removes their footwear before entering the house except for the tabi socks. The samurai footwear consists of sandals called waraji and wooden clogs named geta, and the sandals are from different materials: straw, hemp, and cotton thread. Clogs are usually for the lower class, but sometimes a samurai wears them. On rainy days, the samurai will wear raincoats called kappa made of straw. At times, the samurai may use a folding umbrella made of bamboo slats.

Three young maidens enter with sake containers in their hands. They wear nondescript kimonos to show they are maids. The maids pour sake into each guest's cup, and the women leave to bring in the food.

When the Nightingale Sings

The daimyo claps his hands in delight as his favorite dish appears—three roasted pheasants, with their beautiful plumes used as decoration, raw fish, vinegared vegetables, roasted yams, red beans, grated radish, and broiled fish follow. Individual bowls of steaming clams are next. Fresh persimmons with roasted chestnuts serve as dessert. The men enjoy the delicious fare while indulging in rice wine.

At eight o'clock, Maki enters the room. She goes to her shamisen and begins to play and sing. Maki is tall, willowy, and has a pleasing voice that attracts the men. The men sit and stare at the beautiful courtesan. Sange can see that Daimyo Takayoshi is entranced with Maki's beauty and grace. Sange is pleased that Konoye oka-san is correct—Maki is a perfect hostess.

CHAPTER 8

A sharp rap comes from the front gate. The guard asks who is there. A man around thirty years of age and the height of five feet nine towers over the five-foot four-guard.

"My name is Torakichi. I have come to pay my respect to Lord Sange. Is your master home?"

"He is. Please wait here while I send someone to see if he will meet with you. Koichi, come here."

A lad around eight comes running. Koichi stares at the man at the gate, and looks him over, and looks away.

"Koichi go tell Lord Sange that a man named Torakichi would like to speak to him. Hurry and relay the message."

"Lord Sange! Lord Sange! There is a man named Torakichi at the front gate to see you."

Sange looks surprised.

"Who did you say wanted to see me?"

"A tall man named Torakichi. The man's hair is falling around his shoulders, and he has on a dirty kimono and looks fierce. Torakichi has two swords over his hips."

"Thank you, Koichi. You can run along now. Go to the kitchen and tell the chef to give you some red-bean rice cakes."

Koichi grins and rushes towards the kitchen.

Sange sends a maid to fetch his visitor. Sange pours sake into a cup and slowly sips as he waits.

"You're the same as ever, Sange."

Torakichi looks amused as he bows.

"What are you doing here? How long will you be staying? How is your wife, Akie? You have a daughter, Kimiye. She must be around fifteen."

"My wife and daughter have returned to my in-laws' house because I can no longer care for them. I will stay away as long as it takes me to finish my business," replies Torakichi.

"You will stay here," replies Sange. "What kind of business do you have to finish?"

"My business. I don't want to involve you in something that might bring harm to you and your family. I will stay the night, but I will leave in the morning. Please pour me a cup of sake. If it isn't too much of a bother, I would like something to eat."

Sange claps his hands, and a maid appears. He instructs her to bring more rice wine and food for Torakichi. Sange tells the maid to prepare a room with a futon and pillow for Torakichi's stay. Nori scurries to the kitchen and returns a few minutes later with a tray laden with miso soup, broiled salmon, pickled radish, and rice. Nori pours the sake and leaves.

Sange is in his black kimono, hakama of navy-blue cotton, and a light gray haori with his family crest on its back. Sange's hair is in a topknot and neatly combed over his shaved pate. Torakichi, on the other hand, is dressed in a dirty, faded blue kimono and a worn haori. The family crest on his coat is barely visible. Torakichi's hair is uncombed, and it hangs in disarray to his shoulders. Torakichi has a sword and a short knife attached to a sash at his hip.

Despite the differences in their personalities, the two men are close friends. They sit cross-legged, eyeing each other as they drink their rice wine. Lord Sange's face is expressionless as he touches the top of his shaven pate.

"Don't you ever relax?" asks Torakichi.

"Later," Sange replies. "You are welcome to come to the bathhouse with me. Torakichi, you need a layer of dirt scrubbed off your body. I will give you a change of dress and burn your old clothes."

The two men depart to bathe.

True to Torakichi's word, Sange hears Torakichi leaving in the early morning. Sange wonders where Torakichi is going, and what secrets he is hiding?

Sange is too tired to ponder and turns over and falls back asleep.

Torakichi becomes a ronin after his daimyo casts him out of his samurai clan. Torakichi looks like a vagrant in his clothes and unshaven facial hair and decides to flee before he has to answer any more questions. Torakichi is a disgrace and has nowhere to turn. He does not want to burden Sange with his woes and departs without a word.

Torakichi is ready to serve any daimyo paying wages. Torakichi is strong in martial arts, and the ronin will travel throughout Japan until hired to teach the techniques to new upstarts. Torakichi is homeless, sleeping under the stars or in temples. He chops wood like a common labourer to sustain himself.

The ronin have a reputation for getting into trouble, for joining local fights, for turning into thieves or falling into the world of entertainment. The ronin are known to join samurai clans in need of additional fighters, and some ronin is the source of social and military upheavals. Torakichi swears he will remain a man of honour and not succumb to any devious acts of evil. Torakichi walks to the next village seeking work.

Torakichi is walking eastward, along a river, when teenage boys attack him and throw ripe red tomatoes. Torakichi's new kimono has red splotches all over his back, and the ronin turns and glares at the teens and draws his sword. The boys become frightened and run away.

Torakichi feels a tug on his sleeve. He looks down, and a young boy is trying to wipe away the crushed tomatoes. Torakichi bends down so the boy can reach his shoulders. He smiles at the youngster and bows in thanks.

"What is your name, and how old are you?"

"Everyone calls me, Taizo, and I am ten. I have no parents, and I live under the restaurant over there. I eat the scraps they throw out and do small errands for the owner. I am sorry those mean boys attacked you. They are the village bullies, and they terrorize everyone."

"Are you hungry, Taizo? I have a little money so let's go to the restaurant and eat. Follow me," Torakichi says with a wink.

"I don't know if the owner will welcome me? He might get mad and wonder if I am bothering a patron?"

"The owner might not serve me either. Look at my clothes. I must look like a vagrant?"

Taizo begins to laugh as he merrily says, "Yes, you do look like a homeless person. You are right; they may not serve you either."

"Come along, as long as I have enough coins, they will serve me—I promise."

Torakichi grabs Taizo's hand and walks into the open-air restaurant. A young girl comes running, stops, and glares.

"You cannot come in here. We do not feed the homeless. Taizo, why are you bringing this man here? I am going to tell Mamoru and have you both tossed out."

"Who is Mamoru?" asks Torakichi.

"Mamoru is the owner and cook, and you should be on your way. Mamoru was once a samurai warrior, but his master died. Mamoru knows how to fight with a sword and will end up cutting you."

Torakichi sits in front of a scarred wooden table and tells Taizo to sit in the opposite chair. Taizo has a worried look on his face and begins to shake when he sees Mamoru approaching.

"Mariko tells me she has asked you to leave. Why are you still here? I am busy cooking, and now I have to leave my kitchen to toss you out. I am losing my patience—leave before I have to get my sword," shouts Mamoru angrily.

Torakichi looks at Mamoru with a grin and says, "Hello, Mamoru. Don't you remember me?"

Mamoru is stunned and says, "Torakichi, what are you doing here?"

"The daimyo threw me out of my clan, and my family returned to my in-laws. I have nowhere to go, and I'm picking up odd jobs to keep alive. How have you been? I have coins to pay for our lunch. What is the menu for today?"

"You don't have to pay, my old friend. I will bring you some food. Wait here, and I will have Mariko bring you some sake."

"Wait, I will pay for Taizo's food. I promised Taizo a good meal. Thank you for your kind hospitality, and I will accept your generous lunch, but I must pay for this little lad."

"Torakichi, you have always been an honourable man. All right, you can pay for Taizo's lunch. Just stay here and wait. After you have eaten, I would like to hear about what has happened to you since I last saw you."

Taizo's eyes grow rounder and rounder. He has never seen so much food. Mariko brings in miso soup, and a hot sukiyaki broth, with vegetables and pieces of chicken simmering in an iron pot. Two wooden bowls hold a mound of steaming brown rice, and a small dish contains Japanese pickles. A bowl of fresh plums looks delicious and ripe for dessert. Taizo is stuffing his mouth as fast as he can. Taizo's stomach is growling in delight.

"Slow down, Taizo, or you are going to get a stomachache. There is no hurry. The food is not going to go away. I can order more if this is not enough," says Torakichi.

Taizo slows and rubs his full stomach, and he can hardly breathe. He quickly grabs two plums and hides them in the sleeves of his kimono. Torakichi watches him and shakes his head. Torakichi can't believe this little boy has to resort to hiding some fruit so he won't be hungry later.

"Run along now, Taizo. I have to speak with my old friend Mamoru. I will see you in the morning if you want to come and eat breakfast with me?"

"I will meet you for breakfast, and if you see me sleeping under the restaurant, please wake me. Thank you for the most delicious lunch. It is the best I have ever eaten."

Torakichi watches the boy skip away. He asks Mariko to fetch Mamoru if he is free. Torakichi says he will wait for Mamoru under the peach tree by the river.

Mamoru finds Torakichi fast asleep under the peach tree. He reaches out to shake his friend's shoulder when suddenly, Torakichi leaps to his feet, brandishing his sword.

"Whoa, it is I, Mamoru. You are still as fast as lightning. I'm sorry I woke you. I finished cooking and have a couple of hours before I have to prepare dinner. Would you like some sake? I brought a flask and two cups."

The two men sit down and reminisce about their past as a samurai. Mamoru had been a loyal servant to his daimyo, who died. The clan disassembled, and all the samurai scattered throughout Japan.

Torakichi tells Mamoru, he had been kicked out of his clan by his daimyo, when he had refused to kill a man. The man supposedly had stolen some paintings, but when searched, they could not find any evidence.

Torakichi refused to kill the man without any proof of his evil deed. Torakichi's daimyo had grown angry at Torakichi's refusal and brandished him.

The men talk for several hours. The two friends are from different samurai clans and have lived in separate villages, a short distance from one another. Mamoru and Torakichi have known each other since they were six years of age. The two friends had sworn allegiances to two samurai clans with two different daimyos. The two families lived near each other in peace.

Torakichi meets Taizo for breakfast and gives the boy some coins. Taizo is so grateful he keeps bowing and bowing. Torakichi says he will speak to Mamoru about helping Taizo if he gets into trouble. The ronin thinks he will return for a visit the following year. Torakichi tells Taizo to be a good boy and listen to his elders.

Mamoru decides to adopt Taizo as a favor to Torakichi. Mamoru has always liked the little rascal and wants him as a son. Mamoru informs Torakichi about his plans, and his friend shakes his hand and thanks Mamoru for his kindness. Torakichi says he would have adopted Taizo if his life was more stable. The ronin says he has a long journey to complete before he can return to his own family.

Torakichi feels hopeless, but when he sees other samurai that have lost their masters, he feels a brotherhood. The ronin have no jobs, and they have sold their daggers and swords to be able to eat. He feels lucky he still has his weapons. His brothers were once brave and revered samurai, but now they are only considered beggars. Two days ago, Torakichi had gone to bed on an empty stomach.

Torakichi sees the long lines of ronin on the street ahead. The ronin search for work, but jobs are not plentiful. They are homeless men that are hungry, losing hope. The men that have found jobs carry their handful of possessions, following their new employers.

Torakichi trails behind Tadashi, a farmer who hires him. The forest opens to a meadow near a small mountain, and the farmer and Torakichi reach a bubbling brook and stop to quench their thirst. Torakichi splashes water onto his face and wades into the water to wash his body. The two men continue on the country road through a small village. The farmer and Torakichi approach a house made of bamboo poles and a thatched roof. A woman comes rushing out and looks at Torakichi with interest. She is in a brown kimono, yellow obi, and geta. Her face is full of wrinkles, and she is the farmer's wife.

A large pot of soup is simmering over a fire, and Torakichi's stomach begins to rumble. He hasn't eaten for two days, and the delicious scent almost knocks him over. The farmer looks at Torakichi and asks him if he is hungry, and Torakichi nods his head yes.

"Teruko bring the ronin a bowl of rice and soup. Torakichi will be working in the fields starting tomorrow morning. The man must regain his vigor, or he will be unable to work. After the ronin eats, show him to the stables where he can sleep in one of the stalls. Give Torakichi a blanket and a husk-filled pillow."

Torakichi follows Teruko to the outdoor kitchen, and she scoops soup and rice into a large bowl. Teruko hands Torakichi a small wooden spoon and tells him to sit on a log nearby. Torakichi gulps down the food and eats until the dish is clean. The farmer's wife takes pity on Torakichi and refills the bowl a second time. The ronin thanks Teruko profusely over and over.

Torakichi goes to bed on top of freshly laid hay and covers himself with the futon and lays his head on the pillow. The Ronin's swords are next to him, ready for battle—if necessary. Torakichi is snoring as his exhaustion overcomes him. A nudge of a cold nose from an old nag wakes him in the morning. Torakichi strokes the horse's head and quickly rises.

Breakfast is a rice gruel that is hot and tasty. Torakichi works out in the fields until noon. Teruko brings him rice balls and pickles for lunch. After working until seven, he is ready for dinner and a hot bath. This routine continues for a month, and Torakichi is grateful for his new employer's kindness. Torakichi is a big man and physically fit. He is a good worker, and the farmer is satisfied with his work ethics.

A year goes by, and Torakichi decides to leave. He is going to work on a ship as a deckhand to make more money. Torakichi goes to Yokohama to the shipyards to work and sails between China, Korea, and Japan. The ronin will work for three years and return home.

Torakichi boards a ship called the Red Ruby, and Captain Li and the entire crew dress in loose shirts and tight black pants. The crew's hair is in pigtails, and they wear small round hats that look like discs. The Chinese words, from the crew's mouths, sounds like a singsong tune. The ship is going to Shanghai, a deep-water port and shipping center.

The food aboard the ship is foreign to Torakichi. In the morning, he is served rice porridge and noodles in a broth for lunch. At dinner, they eat fish or meat with sautéed vegetables and fried rice. Torakichi drinks bitter brown tea at every meal. If lucky, Torakichi might get a mandarin orange or an apple. The menu varies at every meal, but it is not always to his liking.

The ship continues along the pitch-black sea, and the Red Ruby travels at a fast pace and flies over the water. Suddenly, the heavens open up, and a pounding rain begins to fall. The sailors keep the ship steady as the rain increases.

The rain stops, and an eerie calm surrounds the ship. The sailors are frightened, and Torakichi is bewildered. From the bowels of the sea, they see something drifting towards their vessel. It looks like floating balls of cotton.

Torakichi shouts, "What is that? What is happening?"

The Chinese sailors are yelling, "Ghostship, Ghostship."

Pandemonium follows as white shapes move towards the ship, and the spirits grow in size. The ghosts are wearing white kimonos, and their hair is dangling on the surface of the water. The spirit's faces illuminate, and their hands reach up over the waves. Torakichi can hear a humming noise and tries to make out the words.

"Lend us a ladle, lend us a hishaku," the spirits are chanting.

Captain Li replies, "No, we will never lend you a spoon, never!"

Torakichi asks, "Why do they want a ladle."

Captain Li replies, "Yurei, or what called ghosts use ladle to swamp boat. If can do this swamping, will come drag us to bottom of ocean. We no can give in to ghost, must get away. Torakichi, give them this ladle. It has holes in it, so no can hold water."

Torakichi goes to the edge of the deck and slips the hishaku into the sea. The ghosts or the yurei, look angry as they realize the spoon is full of holes. The spirits disappear back into the sea, and everyone breathes a sigh of relief, but they know the ghosts will be back.

Suddenly, Torakichi sees a ship approaching and shouts out a warning to Captain Li. The captain does not alter his course and heads right towards the ship. Torakichi begins to yell and wave his hands. The captain looks at Torakichi and dismisses his warning.

The ship is almost on top of them, and Captain Li steers forward. Torakichi's mouth hangs open as the Red Ruby goes right through the phantom ship. Torakichi blinks his eyes in disbelief.

The captain smiles and says, "Yurei ship, ghostship."

Torakichi leans on the deck railing and wipes the perspiration off his face and neck. He never believed in ghosts before—but now—he doesn't know what to think. He saw the yurei in the water, and Torakichi knows, he is not hallucinating because he is wide awake. He can feel his heart beating faster and his pulse racing.

One of the Chinese crewmembers can speak Japanese, and he tells Torakichi about the yureibune or ghostship.

When the Nightingale Sings

"The spirits appear at certain times. We have to be extra careful during stormy weather, foggy nights, and rainy days. A new moon or a full moon is also a time when the yureibune appears. Their goal is to take as many of our souls to increase their numbers. We believe the yurei is a female and not a male.

The ghosts are powerful, and they can appear in other forms. Sometimes as you saw today, it can be a ship. The ghostship came right at our vessel, but Captain Li did not panic and did not deviate from his course. The ghostship was trying to capsize our ship. Did you notice the ghostship had a slight glow? The captain saw and knew the ship was not real.

Many ships wash up with only corpses aboard. Some have living sailors that have become demented from the paranormal experience. Sometimes they lure the ships further out to sea to make them disoriented and off course, and the ghosts take over.

Torakichi, I think many of the crew have been suspicious of you. It is the first time they have ever seen you, and sometimes the ghosts appear as one of the crew. They try to prey on the sailor's emotions. I think today, after seeing your reaction, they no longer think you are a ghost. They saw how pale you became and how you were shaking when you thought the phantom ship was going to kill us.

Another trick of the yurei is to light a bonfire on the open sea. The crews think they are near land. The spirits steer them towards the rocks, and everyone on board will drown. But the ghosts are afraid of a real fire. They will shrink away from a lit lantern, that may throw sparks of fire at them."

"Thank you for explaining this phenomenon to me. It is very frightening. I hope we will not reencounter the ghosts on this trip. I am now a believer that ghosts do exist. I used to laugh at people and thought the people were crazy when they said they saw a ghost. I don't want to encounter any more evil spirits and hope they stay away from our ship. I don't mind meeting some friendly ghosts. There must be some around," responds Torakichi.

Thankfully, the rest of the trip is as usual. No more ghosts appear. Torakichi is thankful nothing happened to his ship and crew. He finds out that many of the sailors are from different parts of China and speak different dialects. Torakichi wants to learn some basic Chinese, but it is going to be difficult when the Chinese themselves are unable to talk to each other. He decides to learn from the sailor that speaks Japanese.

The Port of Shanghai is very busy. It is still mid-afternoon when they are unloading, and Torakichi decides to take a look around the town. There are outdoor stalls selling foods. The ronin decides he is hungry and watches to see what looks good to eat. He sees a small basket with newborn puppies sitting on the ground. Torakichi goes over to take a look when suddenly, a hand reaches into the basket and pulls out one of the puppies. Torakichi steps back and is stunned when a cleaver takes the head off the animal. A customer is standing in front of the stall, nodding her approval. The woman asks for a second puppy as the knife comes down once more.

Torakichi is sick to his stomach. He did not know the Chinese ate dogs. He suddenly becomes worried that the meat dishes he had on board were the meat of dogs. Torakichi stumbles away as nausea sweeps over him. He has lost his appetite and wanders down the road.

People are haggling over prices of merchandise for sale, and the vendors and customers fight. Eventually, they reach an agreement, and the transaction is complete.

Torakichi decides it is time to return to the Red Ruby and eat his dinner. The ship will be leaving port early the next morning. Torakichi is exhausted and wants to get a good night's sleep.

Dreams keep Torakichi awake most of the night, and he sees ghosts hovering over his hammock. He knows these ghosts are not real, but it scares him just the same. Torakichi apologizes to the other crewmembers for keeping them awake, as they glare at him in irritation.

The next morning is a clear day, and the sky is blue, and there are no clouds in the sky. Torakichi is relieved that the ghosts will not come today. He prays the rest of the voyage will continue in good weather.

CHAPTER 9

A young maiden is soaking her left ankle in the cold river water. She tripped and fell over a small rock and hurt herself, and her ankle is now red and swollen. The young girl has long black hair that hangs to her waist. She has almond-shaped brown eyes that look surprised when she sees Masahiro approaching.

Masahiro greets the young maiden, "*Konichiwa,* hello. Have you hurt yourself?"

The girl looks up and looks frightened. She tries to flee, but she falls back onto the ground.

"My name is Masahiro from the Ouchi Clan, and I don't believe we have met. I thought I knew all the young girls from our village, but I don't remember seeing you before. What is your name?"

Masako shyly looks away. She does not want to reveal her real name, so Masako lies and says her name is Kiyoko. Kiyoko is her younger sister's name.

"Kiyoko-san, that is a beautiful name. Kiyoko-san, where do you live? I have never seen you before."

"I live over there."

Masako points to a mountain in the distance.

"You live up on the mountain? What does your family do? Is your father a samurai?"

"No, my father is not a samurai. He is a woodsman. We live on a mountain with three other families. I came down to pick wildflowers and fell. I must hurry home before my family misses me, but I don't know if I can stand."

"Let me help you. Your ankle looks painful. I will find a long stick so you can use it as a cane. Wait here until I return."

Masahiro returns with a long stick and takes out his knife and begins to carve the unwanted protruding knobs. Masahiro helps Masako to stand and hands her the rod to balance herself. Masako thanks Masahiro and says she must be on her way. Pain is causing spasms, and she flinches as she climbs up the mountain.

Masahiro yells out, "Wait!" He goes running towards her as he tears a piece of his kimono. "Let me tie this around your ankle. This fabric should help the swelling go down and stop some of the pain."

Masako thanks Masahiro as she hobbles away.

Masahiro's mother is not happy to see his torn kimono. She asks Masahiro what he was doing to ruin his silk garment.

"You have ruined a silk kimono, and you must not be so careless. The cost of the cloth will feed many mouths. What happened? Where were you?"

"I'm sorry I damaged my kimono. There was a young girl by the river, and she had injured her leg, and I used the cloth to bind her ankle and made her a cane so she could walk home. I'm sorry, Oka-san. I did not do it on purpose, and it was for a good cause."

"Who was the girl?" Is she from Uji? What is her name?"

"Her name is Kiyoko, and she lives on the mountain with her family. She is beautiful, but I have never seen her before. She said her father was a woodsman. That's all I know. I probably will never see her again."

"Masahiro, go and eat your dinner, and I will repair your kimono. I will not be angry since you did a noble deed. I am proud of you!"

"*Arigato*. Thank you. I am so hungry I can eat a bear."

Mitsuko watches her son as he scurries to the dining room. She smiles as she nods her head like a proud parent. Masahiro is growing taller every day, and he is sensitive and kind. Masahiro will make a fine husband one day.

The young master eats his dinner and goes to his room to study. An hour later, he decides to take a bath and go to bed. Masahiro ends up dreaming about Kiyoko, as she dances among the wildflowers in his dream.

In the meantime, Masako is limping home, and it is taking her longer due to the injury. The sun has already set, and she spies her father coming down the path in search.

"Masako, where have you been? Your mother is beside herself with worry. You should have been home hours ago, and you know it is dangerous to be out by yourself after dark. Are you limping? Did you hurt yourself? I will carry you the rest of the way home."

Taiji picks up his daughter as though she is a grain of rice. He is strong because he works in the outdoors. Masako puts her arms around her father's neck and hugs him. After ten minutes, they arrive home, and Shina comes racing out and begins to scold.

"Masako, what happened? You know you are supposed to be home before dark."

"Shina, stop scolding her. She is hurt."

Shina looks troubled as she glances down at her daughter.

"Are you bleeding?"

"No, Masako is not bleeding. She has a sprained ankle. Masako was lucky to meet a young man who bound her ankle and made her a wooden cane. Masako is late because she could not walk or run fast to be home on time. Our daughter will be fine in a few days after she rests her leg. Give Masako some food and tea and put her to bed."

Masako's mind is full of images of Masahiro. Masako decides to go back down to the river to see if she can meet Masahiro again. Masako knows she will have to rest her ankle for at least a week and can hardly wait for her leg to heal.

The following day, Masahiro is practicing his sword fighting in the meadow by the river. He hopes he can see Kiyoko again, but he knows it is impossible. He tries to forget about the beautiful girl, but her face keeps appearing in his mind. He doesn't know what this feeling is about, and Masahiro feels frustrated.

Masahiro goes to the river every day after his studies and pretends he is only there to train in the meadow. Masahiro's thoughts are always of Kiyoko and can't shake it from his mind. If he doesn't see her soon, Masahiro decides he will go up the mountain to find her.

In the meantime, Masako takes off the cloth that is binding her ankle.

"Oka-san, can you please wash this piece of black cloth. It is filthy, and I would like to use it to rebind my ankle. The material is very soft and pleasing to the touch."

Shina picks up the dirty cloth and exclaims, "Masako, this cloth is made of silk, and it is of high quality. You said the boy tore off the piece from the bottom of his kimono? He must be wealthy and must be from a samurai family. Did he tell you his name? I will go down to Uji and personally thank him."

"His name is Masahiro, and I will go with you when I heal. Promise me you will wait until then?"

Shina smiles and nods, "I will wait until you can go with me. Let me see what we can bring as a thank you gift to such a wealthy family."

Shina is lost in her thoughts as Masako frowns.

It is three weeks before Masako can finally walk without a limp. All the cherry blossoms have blown away, and the hot, humid summer is approaching. Masako likes it on the mountain because it is more refreshing than down in the valley. She uses the silk cloth to tie her hair back.

Shina and her daughters are busy making stuffed red-bean rice cakes to sell down at the village. Kiyoko stirs and cools the red-bean paste in a large kettle, and Masako and her mother stuff the cakes with the cooled paste. Kiyoko brings in a wooden container, and they will use a small cart to bring the cakes to the marketplace.

Masako asks her mother if she can take a few rice cakes to Masahiro's house to thank him for his kindness. Shina thinks that is an excellent idea. Shina tells Kiyoko to make a separate package for Masahiro.

When they reach the village, they will inquire where Masahiro lives and drop off the cakes before going to the marketplace. Shina wants to make sure that Masahiro's cakes will be fresh and not left out in the sun in the stall.

Masako, Kiyoko, and their mother reach Uji at three in the afternoon. The sun is beating down, and the humidity is unbearable. They have covered their rice cakes with leaves to keep them moist and fresh. As they reach the bottom of the hill, Masako spots Masahiro with two friends strolling towards them.

Masako whispers to her mother, "Oka-san, Masahiro is walking towards us. He is the tall one in the middle of his friends. What should I do?"

Shina says, "Just wait here until he reaches us, and you can bow and greet him. Don't be shy, just say hello, and give him the rice cakes and say thank you."

"But, what if he turns down another aisle and doesn't come our way?"

"You will have to call out to him, so he notices you. There is no other way. You can't go chasing after him, that is not ladylike."

Masako waits as she watches Masahiro and his friends. He suddenly looks up and stops in surprise. He begins to grin as he steps forward.

Masako bows and says, "*Konichiwa*, hello, I am happy to see you again. We were just going to ask someone where you live. My mother, Kiyoko, and I made red-bean rice cakes this morning, and we wanted to give you some to thank you for your kindness. I'm glad we found you."

Masako hands the package of cakes to Masahiro as she blushes. Masahiro thanks Masako for the gift. Suddenly Masahiro has a frown on his face.

"I don't understand? I thought you said your name was Kiyoko?"

Masako quickly explains, "*Gomenasai*; I apologize, I didn't want to give my name to a stranger. I used my sister's name instead. My name is Masako. I would like you to meet my mother and my younger sister Kiyoko."

Masahiro quickly recovers and introduces them to his friends.

"I would like you to meet my friends—Goro and Takeshi. They are members of our Ouchi Clan. We had a free day from our studies, so we decided to visit the marketplace. It was lucky that we were able to bump into you. Thank you for the rice cakes, they are my favorite food."

Shina bows and says, "Thank you again for helping Masako. We have to be on our way. We have brought a container of rice cakes to sell."

Masahiro doesn't want Masako to go and asks if she is free to meet at the teahouse at four. Shina smiles and says it will be fine. The family will not be leaving until they sell all their cakes. Shina thinks it will take a couple of hours, and Masako should be back at their stall by six. Masahiro says he will make certain Masako is back in time.

Masahiro tells his friends he is meeting Masako for tea, and he doesn't want them to go with him. Goro laughs and pushes him playfully.

"I thought friends are supposed to share," Takeshi laughs.

"I'll see you tomorrow," says Masahiro as he grins.

Masahiro walks down the stalls. He is looking for a small gift for Masako. He finds a little shop that has ribbons and trinkets and picks a pink silk ribbon for Masako to wear in her hair.

"A pleasure to serve you. Please come again," bows a young seller as she looks at the handsome stranger.

When Masako arrives at the teahouse, she notices Masahiro's friends are no longer with him.

"Where are your friends? Are they coming later?"

"No, Goro and Takeshi have gone home. I didn't want to share you with them, and I wanted to talk to you alone. How is your leg? Is it completely healed? It is good to see you again, and I hope we can meet from time to time. I go to the river once a day to practice my sword fighting, and perhaps you can meet me there. I am usually there around three," says Masahiro.

"I don't come down from the mountain very often. I have to help my mother with chores. I can manage to go to the river once a week, but I can't tell you which day, so I don't want you to wait for me," responds Masako.

Masahiro replies, "It doesn't matter what day you can come. I will be there every day, and if for some reason I am not there, please do not panic. I probably have something I must do for my own family. Hopefully, we can meet sometime next week."

Masako and Masahiro enjoy their green tea, and they find they can converse comfortably, as the time they spend together slip away. To Masahiro being with Masako is like a dream come true. Masahiro notices the black silk cloth binding her long black hair and is pleased. Masako blushes as she tries to explain.

"I love the feel of the silk you gave me, and I didn't want to throw it away. It would be a waste. I hope you don't mind me using it to tie my hair?"

"It is a wonderful idea. The silk looks beautiful against your hair, and I'm glad you have found another use for it. My mother was a little miffed at me for tearing my kimono. After I explained the situation, she said she was proud of me. She repaired my kimono by adding a strip of black silk, and it looks brand new."

"I bought you a small gift. I hope you like it," says Masahiro.

Masako is thrilled. She ties the pink silk ribbon onto her hair.

Masako looks at Masahiro and says, "Arigato, it is beautiful. Now I have two ribbons you have given me. I have given you nothing, so what should I do?"

Masahiro says, "You have given me your friendship. That is all I need."

Masahiro walks Masako back to her mother's stall. He whispers to Masako not to forget about meeting him by the river the following week. Masahiro bows and bids farewell to Shina and Kiyoko. Masahiro turns and waves, and Masako smiles in happiness as she waves back.

Shina watches Masako's face and shakes her head because there is no possibility that Masako can marry Masahiro. He is a samurai. Masako's family is poor, and Masako's father is a woodsman, and Shina is a seller of foods in the village marketplace. Masahiro's parents will never agree to have their precious son marry into a lower-class family. Shina feels sorry for her daughter and decides to warn Masako before the relationship becomes more intense.

After eating supper, Masako's father goes to take a bath. Kiyoko is busy feeding the animals in the barn. Shina decides this is the perfect time to confront Masako about Masahiro.

"Masako, I need to speak with you. I want to warn you that your relationship with the young samurai is forbidden. Masahiro is from a prestigious family and is very wealthy, and his parents will not condone your friendship. If they find out you are seeing Masahiro, they will step in and forbid him to continue to meet. I'm sorry you were not born into a family of wealth. You are my daughter, and I cherish you. It is best if you never see Masahiro again. It will be less hurtful for both of you before your relationship goes any further."

"I understand, Oka-san. I know I should not meet Masahiro again. I have one favor to ask, and that is, I would like to meet Masahiro for one last time. We have plans to meet sometime next week by the river, and I will pretend nothing is amiss and enjoy the afternoon. I will not tell Masahiro this meeting will be the last, and he will give up waiting for me when I do not show up at the river again. I think that is the best way to put this relationship to rest."

Shina agrees and tells Masako she is sorry that their family is so desolate and impoverished. If Shina could change anything, she would sacrifice her own life to make Masako happy. Masako and Shina cling together as their tears flow down their cheeks. Masako goes to bed and hopes she can at least have dreams of Masahiro.

Masahiro goes to the river for three days. On the fourth day, he laughs in joy as he spots Masako dipping her bare feet into the cold water.

"You're here. I'm happy to see you. How long can you stay?"

"I can stay for two hours, and then I have to go home before it becomes dark. I'm happy to see you too, and you must be busy training every day. It is my honour to have a friend that is a samurai."

Masahiro sits on the ground and begins to make a bracelet out of the wildflowers at his feet. Masahiro hands Masako his artistic gift and smiles as she places it around her wrist.

"*Domo-arigato*, thank you. It is beautiful. I will dry the flowers and leave it by my bed. Thank you again, and I wish I had something to give you."

Masako searches the ground and spies a beautifully shaped stone. She picks it up and hands it to Masahiro.

"Please accept this little gift. Rub it to remember me, and it will calm you. I hope you like it?"

Masahiro gently rubs the stone and says, "I can already feel the calming effect. I will always think about you when I touch this stone. *Domo-arigato.*"

Two hours later, Masako has to leave. She says goodbye to Masahiro and begins to walk up the mountain path. Masahiro shouts to Masako to remind her he will be waiting at the river the following week. Masahiro does not see the tears streaming down Masako's face. Masako is devastated that she will never come down to the river again. Masahiro smiles as he turns for home. He is anticipating meeting Masako once more. If Masahiro knew this was their final meeting, Masahiro would never have agreed to their parting.

Masahiro doesn't know why Masako has not appeared at the river. He worries that she might be hurt or ill. Masahiro decides to send one of his male servants to search for Masako's home. After waiting for hours, he sees Kenji returning.

"Did you find Masako? Is she well? Hurry and tell me what you found?"

"Your friend is well. I spoke with her mother, and she has forbidden her daughter from seeing you again. Her mother said you are a samurai and from an elite Japanese family, and her daughter is only a poor woodsman's offspring. The mother fears that your family will brandish you from your home, and her daughter would be the cause. She did not want your relationship to go any further to cause a rift between you and your parents. Masako's mother says she is sorry, but she needs to protect her daughter as well."

Masahiro loses his footing and stumbles back. He knows his servant is right. His parents will forbid Masahiro from seeing a girl below their social status. Masahiro has fallen in love with Masako, and he doesn't want to lose her. Masahiro decides his only choice is to speak to his grandfather and receive his advice.

"Grandfather, may I have a few words with you? I have a big burden on my shoulders, and I think you are the only one to relieve it."

"What is the matter, Masahiro? Did you do something wrong? Quickly tell me so I can fix it."

"The only wrong I have done is to fall in love with a girl below my station. She lives on the mountain with her family. Masako's father is a woodsman, and her mother sells rice cakes down in the marketplace. They are poor. Masako's mother has forbidden Masako to see me again. She says she is protecting her daughter as well as me. Masako's mother fears my parents will disown me and brandish me from our home. Do you have any advice you can give to me?"

"Oh my," replies Mito. "I don't know what we can do. I will speak to your father, but your mother will make the final decision. I don't think your parents will permit you to see the girl. You best forget about her.

Your parents will find a nice pretty girl from another samurai family for you to marry."

"I will not marry if I cannot wed Masako. I will relinquish being a samurai warrior and become a monk. I do not desire another woman, and I will never agree to a fixed marriage. You can tell that to my parents."

Masahiro wipes the tears from his face as he stalks away in anger.

Mito is in a quandary and goes to find his son.

"Sange, I need to discuss something important immediately."

"What is it? Can it wait? I am writing a letter to the daimyo. Give me ten minutes, and I will meet you in the garden where we can have tea."

Mito paces back and forth and watches the koi as they leap from the pond hoping for food. Mito loves his grandson dearly and wants all the happiness for Masahiro. Mito doesn't know if he will be able to grant Masahiro his one wish, a wife that is poor and has no social status. Mito sighs as he spots an owl sitting on a branch of a red maple tree. Mito looks up as he hears Sange's footsteps.

Sange claps his hands, and a maid appears with the makings of tea. She whisks the powdered tea with hot water and hands the cups to the waiting men. She leaves a plate of ogashi, a sweet confection, and departs.

Sange motions his father to sit down on the cushions overlooking the garden. Sange's father looks so glum he becomes worried.

"You are not ill, are you? You don't look happy. What has happened to make you this way?"

"I am here to speak on behalf of your son. Masahiro is very unhappy. He has fallen deeply in love with a girl named Masako. She is a poor woodsman's daughter, and she is not someone you and Mitsuko will welcome as a daughter-in-law. Masahiro has threatened he will marry no other, and If he cannot marry this girl, he will become a monk. What shall we do?"

Sange is shocked. He calls for his wife.

"Mitsuko, my father tells me Masahiro has fallen in love with a girl named Masako. If he cannot marry her, Masahiro will become a monk. Masahiro will not agree to an arranged marriage and will resign from the Ouchi Clan."

"Masako, you say. I think she is the girl that was hurt down by the river. Masahiro tore off the hem of his kimono and bound her sprained ankle. Masahiro made her a cane out of a tall stick he found on the ground. I did not know Masahiro was still meeting Masako. We must change Masahiro's mind and have him agree to stop seeing this girl."

Mito replies, "I think it is too late. Masahiro is so obsessed with this girl he can't think straight. Anything you say will only make Masahiro want her more. We need a distraction. Perhaps you can arrange for Masahiro to meet some of the available samurai daughters. What do you say if we hold a small party as a ruse? Mitsuko, can you check out the samurai daughters and see if you can find one beauty that might catch Masahiro's eye? The get together is our only chance to change Masahiro's mind, and we better set the party as soon as possible. How about sometime next week?"

Both of Masahiro's parents agree to have a party. Mitsuko sets the event in motion, and she invites several samurai daughters and invites Masahiro's samurai friends. She wants to make it look as though it is just a small insignificant gathering.

Takeshi and Goro are the first to arrive, and Masahiro greets them at the door and ushers them inside. A maid brings in Tadashi and Ichiro. Next to come is Noboru, Satoshi, and Kenji.

"Where are the women? I thought the invitation said we were going to have a party. I saw Nobuko yesterday, and she said she was coming," Goro questions.

"My mother showed me the guest list, but I didn't pay much attention. I remember one name, I think it was Sachiko," replies Masahiro.

The men become quiet as the women begin to arrive. The women have on colourful silk kimonos with their long black hair reaching towards the floor. After everyone is present, Mitsuko introduces everyone. Mitsuko has invited women from other clans, so everyone is not familiar with one another. After Mitsuko introduces all of Masahiro's samurai friends, she presents all the invited women.

"I would like to introduce the women from the various samurai clans in this area. I think everyone knows Nobuko-sama from our own Ouchi Clan. Next to her is Sachiko-sama from the Toji Clan in the next village. Hiroko-sama and Yuki-sama are twin sisters also from the Toji Clan. Sadako-sama, Iriko-sama, Hoshi-sama, and Tomiko-sama are from the Mizu Clan to the south of Uji. I welcome all of you tonight, and I am pleased you were able to attend. I know all your parents and have assured them this party will be honourable. Please enjoy the food and entertainment that will follow. After the party, your clan guards will come to take you home."

Masahiro notices one of the girls is eyeing him and seems to be flirting. Masahiro doesn't remember her name and looks away.

Mitsuko asks everyone to be seated for dinner, and she places the men on one side and the women on the other side of the tables. Mitsuko claps her hands, and the maids open the shoji doors and enter bringing in the banquet. The first course is a clear soup with a drop of a quail's egg in the middle, and the next course is a vinegared dish of sliced cucumbers and carrots. There is an exclamation of approval as a large barbecued pig arrives. Prawns and vegetable tempura grace the table. A large platter of seafood sashimi follows.

The banquet continues with little interaction between men and women. Mitsuko becomes worried and decides to intervene. Mitsuko asks everyone to follow her to the garden and brings out a basket with prewritten questions. Mitsuko tells everyone they are going to play a little game. Yuki is the first woman chosen to start the game.

Yuki reaches into the basket and pulls out a paper with a man's name at the top. Yuki must ask the named man the question on the paper. Yuki looks puzzled, and Mitsuko tells her to read the question.

"Goro-san, do you have a cat?"

Mitsuko tells Yuki she must go sit down next to Goro and receive his answer. Eventually, all the women pick a question and are soon seated next to one of the men. After a few minutes, there are excited voices as the men and women begin to interact. All the shyness of the evening is gone, and the men and women are finally enjoying each other's company. Mitsuko sighs in relief and exits from the party.

Sadako has drawn Masahiro's name. She is excited. She knows he is from a renowned samurai family, and her parents would be happy she is interacting with him. Sadako is petite with a vivacious personality. She is wearing a peach silk kimono with a green obi. Her silky black hair is tied back with a green ribbon that matches her obi sash. She finds Masahiro to be kind and gentle. He asks if she would like a tour of the garden. She happily accepts.

The party is soon over. Their guards escort the women home. The men linger, discussing the women they have met.

"Masahiro, Sadako-san seemed to be interested in you. She is a pretty girl. I would be thrilled if she would look at me like she does you," Tadashi says.

"I'm not interested in any of the women that were here tonight. They are all from good families, and each one is well mannered, and they are all beautiful in their way. I like someone else, and I want to marry her someday. I don't know if that will be possible because she is not from our world. She lives up on the mountain and lives with her sister and parents. I don't think my parents will give me their permission to marry someone below my station. I don't know what to do?"

Masahiro's friends look at him sympathetically. They pat his shoulders as they leave.

Tadashi turns and says, "Does that mean you won't mind if I pursue Sadako-san?"

"Yes, you have my permission to pursue Sadako-san. I wish you good luck. She is a wonderful person, and Sadako-san could not find a better man than you."

Masahiro steps into the garden and looks up at the heavens and searches the stars. The quarter moon is accenting the sky, and Masahiro sits down on the steps of the garden and begins to weep.

Nori is watching Masahiro's grief. She goes to tell her mistress of what she has just witnessed.

"Your son is in the garden. Masahiro is crying. I did not want to interrupt his sorrow, so I came to tell you. I think someone should go and comfort him."

Mitsuko goes in search of Sange and Mito. They are playing a game of Go, and Mitsuko can hear the sound of laughter as they drink their sake. Mitsuko knocks on the closed door and enters.

"I am sorry to disturb your game. One of the maids informed me Masahiro is in the garden weeping. I don't think the party tonight was helpful, and my son is still thinking about Masako. I think we should leave Masahiro alone and not interfere at this time. If we go against Masahiro, he will rebel. Give me a solution if you have any. This entire situation is breaking my heart."

Mito shakes his head and says, "My poor grandson. What are we going to do? I think you are right, Mitsuko, and we will pretend that nothing is wrong. Masahiro needs to clear his head, and I think we should send him away for a while. Sange, you can go with him on a pilgrimage. Take Masahiro to Mt. Koya and camp out under the stars. A visit to the shrine will do some good, and you can leave the day after tomorrow."

CHAPTER 10

Sange and Masahiro arrive at the foot of Mt Koya. The two men dismount from their horses and decide to eat their obento near a stream. The elevation of the mountain is 2,953 feet or 900 meters. Eight low peaks surround it, and the cedar trees are very dense.

Sange explains to Masahiro about the founder.

"Kobo Daishi erected the monastic buildings in 816. It is high on the mountain to avoid distractions from everyday life. Daishi was the founder of Shingon Buddhism in Japan. He lived and taught in Koyasan for nineteen years before he entered eternal meditation in 835. His mausoleum is said to give aid and comfort to those who pray to him.

Dai Garan is eight buildings. It is a quiet and secluded place where Buddhist monks can gather and practice. The monks study, train, and learn the ritual of Shingon Buddhist. They have done this since the ninth century."

Masahiro and Sange sit down to their first dinner with the monks. The monks are vegetarians, and the courses consist of five flavors, five cooking methods, and five colours. The meals have a grilled dish, a deep-fried dish, a pickled dish, a tofu dish, and a soup dish. They will eat with the monks for the next few days. The meals will cleanse their systems.

Masahiro is thrilled to be on the mountain. He will get a taste of living like a monk if he ever decides to become one. If Masahiro cannot marry Masako, he will leave his grandiose life and live a humble life as a monk. Masahiro is looking forward to this entire adventure with his father.

The following day, a young monk welcomes Sange and Masahiro, and the two travelers take off their footwear and enter the monastery. It is lunchtime. The monks serve steamed rice, pickled radish, miso soup, vegetable tempura, hijiki seaweed, cold tofu, and cooked pumpkin.

Sange and Masahiro attend the fire ritual to destroy negative energies, evil thoughts, and desires, and to ask for blessings. A monk is seated in front of the shrine and begins to perform. The brother sets up a woodpile to burn written prayers. The monk lights the fire, and the fire keeps growing higher and higher towards the sky.

Sange and Masahiro take a hot bath and go to bed.

The next morning, at six-thirty, the monks are chanting. They are striking the cymbals and drums. Smoke from the incense pots is rising in the air, and Sange and Masahiro bow as they throw incense into the burning bowl.

After a light breakfast of okaiyu, a rice gruel, and salted red plum, Sange and Masahiro decide to stroll the temple grounds. The grounds look immaculate with several gardens and a koi pond. The two men join a meditation class.

Lunch is a bowl of soba noodles in a rich broth, and the buckwheat noodles are cold and delicious. Fresh oranges are in a small basket, and the two men drink brown herbal tea.

Sange takes Masahiro to the outdoor onsen. The volcanic hot springs are healing and refreshing.

In the afternoon, Sange and Masahiro visit the Okuno-in Buddhist Cemetery. They say their prayers and look at all the tombstones lined in a row.

Masahiro finds himself alone walking back to the temple from the Kobo Daishi's mausoleum. His father decides to stay behind at the temple to pray. Masahiro is walking down the path, and he suddenly feels a chill. A few hours earlier, when the sun was still shining, it was peaceful and serene as Masahiro moved through the cemetery, now he sees lit lanterns along the pathway. He stops and listens to the sound of a geta coming down the roadway. Masahiro thinks it might be a priest and stops and waits until the footsteps halt directly behind him. Masahiro bows, and turns, to greet the monk. He looks up and is surprised no one is there. The young warrior looks up and down the empty pathway. Masahiro suddenly is frightened and races back to the temple to tell his father.

Sange watches Masahiro with a keen eye. He hopes Masahiro is not depressed and thinking about Masako. Sange is relieved when he sees no signs of any depression from his son's eyes. The cold mountain air seems to revive Masahiro, and Masahiro appears to enjoy spending the time with his father. Sange was going to ask his son about Masako, but he decides to let well enough alone.

Mitsuko visits Masako's family while her husband and son are on their trip to Mt. Koya. Mitsuko wants to explain to Masako's parents why the two children cannot be together. She takes Kenji, the servant, who knows where Masako lives. Kenji had previously found Masako's home for Masahiro on the mountain.

Kenji knocks on the door, and Shina answers. Mitsuko thinks Shina is quite beautiful, with her long black hair tied back with a ribbon.

"Konnichiwa, good day. Are you lost and looking for someone?" asks Shina.

Mitsuko replies, "Are you Masako-san's mother?"

"Yes, I am. May I ask who you are?" answers Shina politely.

"My name is Mitsuko, and your daughter knows my son Masahiro. My son believes he is in love with your daughter, but I have told him it is impossible to continue the relationship. I have nothing against your daughter, but Masahiro must marry someone in the samurai family. I hope you understand?"

"I have already forbidden Masako to meet your son. I have stopped her from going down to the river where she says he practices with his swords. Masako knows her place, and you don't have to worry about her any longer. I think it would be best to tell your son that my daughter has no interest in prolonging their friendship. I know it took a lot of courage for you to come to my home today. I understand your dilemma, and my heart breaks for both of the children. I wish they could be together, but I know it is impossible. I just pray they will be able to accept the inevitable?"

Mitsuko beckons to her servant. Kenji hands her a furoshiki, and the silk cloth wrap has beautiful scenes of geese. Mitsuko presents it to Shina and bows.

"Please accept this small gift. Inside are small anchovies that you can use in cooking. I am sorry to have disturbed you, and thank you for your understanding. I find you to be a very gracious lady, and I'm certain your daughter must be like you. I only wish we did not have these social rules. Thank you, and I will be on my way."

Shina bows in thanks, and goes back into the house, and finds Masako standing behind the door listening to Masahiro's mother. Tears are streaming down Masako's face, and she runs sobbing to her room. Shina calmly goes into the kitchen and unwraps the anchovies and places them into a shallow basket.

After days of meditation and praying, Sange and Masahiro decide to go home. The monks give them an obento box, and they thank them for their thoughtfulness. They walk down the path to the stables to retrieve their horses. Sange and Masahiro reach home as the rain begins to fall.

Mitsuko is relieved to see Masahiro in good spirits. He seems to be a different person from when he left, and her son is happier and more animated. Masahiro hugs his mother and goes to take a bath. Masahiro is exhausted from the long trip, and he quickly falls asleep. The young master does not dream.

Weeks speed by, and Masako does her chores without complaining. Masako loses weight, and her face becomes pale. Masako mopes around the house and rarely goes outside. Kiyoko asks her to go on a picnic in the woods, and Masako says she has no interest and refuses. Shina and Taiji worry about their daughter.

"Taiji, I think we must resolve this situation between Masako and Masahiro. I think it is time to divulge our secret because I cannot watch Masako suffer any longer. I am going down to Uji and tell

Masahiro's mother everything. Please don't try to stop me. I am going first thing tomorrow morning."

Taiji agrees with his wife and goes to bed.

The next morning, Shina goes down to the village and finds Masahiro's home, and knocks on the gate. A guard opens the gate and glares at her.

"We do not want anyone selling their goods at our door. Be on your way. This house is a private samurai residence."

"I have come to see Mitsuko-sama. She will see me if you tell her Shina is at the gate and wants to see her about an important matter. I will wait here for her answer."

The guard does not know if he should bother his mistress. He decides to notify a maid about Shina. Nori rushes to Mitsuko's bedchamber and tells her a woman named Shina is waiting outside.

Mitsuko tells Nori to bring her inside. Mitsuko is surprised and wonders what has happened to make Shina come to her home.

"*Ohayo-gozaimasu*, good morning, what brings you to my home? You look rather shaken and serious. Did something happen to our children?"

"I don't know where to begin. I guess I will have to start at the beginning. Perhaps if your husband is at home, he should hear this too?"

"I will have Sange brought here."

Mitsuko sends Nori to get Sange and requests to have tea brought in with some confectionary. Mitsuko motions for Shina to sit, and Sange comes into the room looking worried.

"I am going to tell you a rather long tale. It is a true story that Taiji and I have kept a secret for fifteen years. Empress Kanaye died giving birth to Princess Akiko, as Emperor Morihito lay dying from his injuries during the rebellion. I was Empress Kanaye's Lady-in-waiting, and Taiji was the Captain of the Guards, and the emperor ordered us to take the princess and flee. I have come to confess that Masako is, in reality, Princess Akiko. Masako loves your son so much; I worry my daughter might commit suicide if she cannot marry your son. I hope you believe me, but if you do not, I brought Princess Akiko's royal baby kimono for you to see."

Shina opens a beautiful silk furoshiki square fabric and takes out the elaborate royal kimono. Inside there is also a solid gold bracelet.

Mitsuko gasps, and Sange lets out a sigh. They can't believe what they are hearing. Masako is Princess Akiko? Now Masahiro cannot live up to the standard of a royal. Mitsuko begins to laugh at the absurdity of their new situation.

"Are you saying your daughter can marry my son? He is a samurai, but your daughter is a princess. Now the shoe seems to be on the other foot. What do you suggest we do?" asks Mitsuko.

"I think we should let Masahiro and Masako marry. We can tell everyone Masako is the daughter of a samurai and has lived with us due to unusual circumstances. Would that be all right with you?" Shina questions.

"Does Masako know that she is, in reality, a princess?" questions Sange.

"No, we have never told her. If Masako knew she would not be struggling with this situation with your son. Do you want me to tell Masako, or do you want to keep it a secret? I think it would be for the best if Masako thinks she is a daughter of a samurai that died. I can tell my daughter I was a maid in their household and became her guardian when her mother died at childbirth. What do you think we should do?"

Sange and Mitsuko are at a loss for words. Their son has fallen in love with a princess.

Mitsuko says, "I guess our son knows quality when he sees it. I can't believe she is Princess Akiko, and I thought all the royals were dead. What do you want, to do Sange? Masahiro will be elated to find out he can marry Masako."

Sange replies, "I better confer with my father. I will ask him to come."

Sange turns to Shina and asks her to be patient and wait until his father arrives. The entire problem needs

Mito's approval, since Mito is the patriarch of the family, and his word is the final say.

Shina nods her head in agreement. They hear footsteps outside the corridor. The maid knocks and opens the door, and Mito enters and looks surprised to see a visitor.

"What is so important that the matter cannot wait? I was eating a late breakfast. May I ask who this lovely visitor is?"

Mitsuko introduces Shina and tells Mito the message she has brought. Mito's eyes grow larger as he seems to be in shock.

"Is this true? Is your daughter Princess Akiko?"

Mitsuko hands Mito the royal garment and the gold bracelet. Mito is stunned, but now he believes.

"Mitsuko and I would like your words of wisdom, Father. We cannot decide this by ourselves. Shall we allow Masahiro to wed Masako? I mean Princess Akiko?"

Mito is in deep thought.

"Do you three still plan to deceive them with your tale? I think it would be best to tell them the truth. Masahiro and Masako will have to keep it a secret. I will not be a part of the deceit. Up to now, you had to protect your ward, but now it is time to let my grandson protect her. It is my decision, and in good conscience, I will not deviate from it."

Sange, Mitsuko, and Shina agree Mito is right. They decide to have Masahiro and Masako meet later in the evening. It will be a huge surprise, but they believe telling the truth will be the best. Everyone agrees.

CHAPTER 11

In the year 1640, Empress Kanaye gives birth to a baby girl. After eighteen hours of hard labour, the empress passes away. During this time, there is a coup, and Emperor Morihito is defeated and injured. As the emperor lies on his deathbed, he orders his wife's Lady in Waiting, Shina, and Taiji, his Captain of the Guards, to take the newborn baby and flee.

Taiji leads Shina and the baby out through a secret tunnel carrying a small torch to light the way. The ground is muddy, and rats scurry here and there. Shina holds the royal baby tightly in her arms as they run. The couple does not have time to gather any clothing, food, or drinks. The enemy is already in the palace, and they barely escape.

Taiji has to lift Shina through an opening at the end of the tunnel. Taiji hands Shina the baby as she struggles to keep her balance. Taiji throws a rope to Shina and tells her to tie it around a sturdy tree so he can heave himself up. After reaching the forest, the pair look back at a blazing scene. The palace is burning, and red embers are shooting onto the ground. Taiji and Shina hurry along the path until they reach the forest. To their amazement, the couple finds two horses and some supplies tied to a tall pine tree. Shina fastens the baby on her back with a strip of fabric torn from the hem of her kimono. Shina and Taiji mount the horses and gallop up the mountainside. The side-by-side rhythm keeps the princess asleep.

After an hour's ride, they stop by a small stream to rest. Shina opens the supplies and finds bronze, silver, and gold coins in different denominations. There is also clothing for the princess, but there is no food or milk.

Princess Akiko begins to awaken. She makes small sucking sounds as her tiny mouth searches for nourishment. Shina cannot nurse the baby and doesn't know what to do? Taiji tells her to sit on a log and wait. He will try to find milk and food.

Taiji spots smoke coming out of a chimney as he climbs upwards. Taiji sees the light inside a log cabin, and a man is outside tending to his horse. Taiji shouts out a greeting so as not to scare him.

"*Konbanwa*. Good evening! My wife and I are lost. We have our daughter, a newborn with us. Can you spare us some food and milk? They are waiting for my return at the bottom of the hill."

The man looks startled to see another human being on the mountain.

The man peers suspiciously at Taiji and says, "I can give you some goat's milk. Will that do?"

"That would be wonderful, *domo arigato gozaimasu*. Thank you very much. I have a few coins that I can give you in payment. I also would need a spoon to feed the baby the milk. Unfortunately, my wife cannot produce her milk, and a surrogate maid was nursing our daughter when we were at home. Some rebels came to our estate and robbed us and turned us out. My name is Taiji."

"I am called Saburo. I live here by myself. My wife died a year ago, and we did not have any children. Please go and get your wife and baby and bring them to my cabin. It is already dark and chilly. The altitude is higher here than down at the village, making it colder."

Taiji brings Shina and the baby to the cabin. The woodsman has a pot of stew simmering over the fireplace. Saburo milked his goat while Taiji left to get Shina and the baby. Shina slowly spoons the warm milk into the baby's mouth. Saburo gets three bowls and fills them with the stew, and Shina and Taiji are so hungry they gratefully eat the hot meal.

Saburo tells Shina she is about the same size as his deceased wife. He opens a trunk and begins to take out some old kimonos. Saburo says Shina is welcome to use any of the garments in the chest. Shina is grateful for his generosity and finds some fabric to make makeshift diapers.

Saburo gives Shina and the baby his bed to sleep, and he and Taiji sleep on the floor. The following morning the woodsman is up early making breakfast. Saburo is making gruel out of rice bran. Shina watches Saburo crack an egg and add a bit of precious salt to the simmering pot.

Shina blows on the gruel to cool it before she eats and tries to spoon the broth from the porridge into the baby's mouth. The baby seems to enjoy the porridge broth and opens her mouth for more. Shina speaks to the baby in soothing tones. After changing diapers and a few more mouthfuls of milk, the baby blissfully falls asleep.

Taiji speaks, "Do you think it would be possible to build a little house and stay here on the mountain? I think it is a lovely place to live. Shina, what do you think? Saburo, how about you? Will you help us erect a little house?"

Saburo is elated. The woodsman was lonely living on the mountain alone. Saburo will love to have company and says he will help build a new house nearby. They can start that very day if Taiji helps him finish some of his chores. Saburo will teach Taiji and Shina how to survive.

Taiji and Saburo build a small cabin with two bedrooms, a kitchen, and an outhouse within walking distance. Shina and Taiji share a bathhouse with Saburo. Shina becomes pregnant, and Kiyoko is born. Masako dotes on the new baby, and they thrive in the beautiful world of nature. Taiji becomes a woodsman, farmer, devoted husband, and father. Shina is an excellent cook, and she makes red-bean rice cakes to sell in the village. The two girls take lessons at home from Shina and Taiji—both well-educated and excellent teachers.

One day when Masako is twelve and Kiyoko ten, Taiji decides to teach the girls the art of throwing small knives to defend themselves. Taiji also wants to teach them the art of sword fighting. Shina knows this is something they need to be proficient at and quickly agrees. Every day after dinner, they practice, and Saburo comes outside and watches the three people he has grown to love. One day, Saburo makes three sticks out of bamboo to be used to practice kendo. Masako is a natural and quickly becomes an excellent swordswoman, and Taiji is proud and rewards Masako. Taiji whittles a wooden bee as a gift. This bee becomes Masako's most treasured possession.

Masako learns how to extract honey from the beehives. She waits until the bees leave their nests, and Masako uses a sharp knife to slice off some of the honeycombs. The bees will be gone for hours searching for nectar. Shina makes candles from the wax and uses the honey as a sweetener. Shina uses the honey to make medicine, and the bees help to pollinate their crops. Somehow the bees sense Masako means no harm, and she is never stung. Masako can stand in front of the hive with her hands outstretched with the bees buzzing around her.

A year later, another couple wanders onto the mountainside, and they are seeking a new life and a new place to live. The couple decides they would like to live alongside Saburo and Taiji's family. Their names are Kenji and Matsue. They have come from the island of Kyushu in the most southern part of Japan, and Kenji is a blacksmith and his wife a seamstress. Kenji goes to Uji and finds work with an overworked blacksmith. Matsue goes from door to door seeking employment among the wealthy. Matsue only needs to find one woman that will give her a chance to make her magnificent clothing. After that, word of mouth should get Matsue to other clients.

Masako is growing into a gorgeous woman. She is tall and slender, and her silky hair cascades downwards past her waist. Masako is now fifteen and an excellent sword fighter. She can throw a small knife, twenty feet with accuracy. Masako goes down the mountainside, to a river by a beautiful meadow, whenever she has free time. The lake is where Masako slips and falls on a slippery stone, and Masahiro finds her soaking her injured ankle.

CHAPTER 12

Shina returns home to take Masako to Masahiro's home. She tells Taiji she has discussed Masako's past with Mitsuko, Sange, and Mito. Shina says they are going tell the two children who Masako is. If they want to marry, it is all right with Masahiro's family. Shina wants to know if it is all right with Taiji.

"It is fine with me. Everyone in the two families will know the truth. We will still have to tell a lie and say Masako is from a samurai family, and her daimyo killed. We can never divulge the fact she is Princess Akiko. If someone outside finds out Masako is the princess, they will try to kill her. Please, Shina, let us protect her even if we live a lie."

"Yes, I am aware of the danger. I know Masahiro's family understands too. Do you want to go with me to their home when I bring Masako?"

"Are we going to tell Kiyoko? I think we should wait until she is older. We can ask Matsue to watch over her while we are visiting Masahiro's family. Kiyoko loves to sew, so Matsue can help her make a new kimono."

"I will ask Matsue if she has time to instruct Kiyoko tonight. I will give Kiyoko that beautiful silk fabric that she admires so much. Please tell Masako we are going to Uji this evening to meet with Masahiro's family. She will be curious and will want to know the reason. Tell Masako she will find out in good time and will be happy with the outcome."

Taiji, Shina, and Masako arrive at Masahiro's home at seven. Masako is excited but does not know what is going on? Masako is apprehensive as her father asks the gatekeeper to announce their arrival. The family is ushered to the house and sits in front of a beautifully landscaped garden. A maid appears with tea and a small plate of candy. After a few minutes, Mitsuko, Sange, Mito, and Masahiro arrive.

"*Konbanwa.* Good evening. We are happy to see you again. May I introduce you to our son Masahiro. I believe you have met him before, and this must be Masako-sama. Thank you for coming to see us tonight. We have some important matters to discuss," remarks Sange.

Shina takes the lead and explains the entire story to Masako and Masahiro. They both look stunned with the news. Shina goes on to explain that it must be a secret and never divulged that Masako is Princess Akiko. Shina informs Masahiro and Masako that the two families have agreed to their marriage if they want to wed.

Masahiro replies, "Yes, I would like to marry your daughter. I love her very much, and I missed her while we were separated. I hope Masako feels the same way towards me?"

Masahiro looks at Masako with longing. He is frightened she may refuse his proposal. There is complete silence as they wait for Masako to answer.

"Yes, I would like to marry Masahiro. Thank you for telling us the truth. I would like to continue to be called Masako and not Akiko. Let us say Princess Akiko is dead."

Everyone nods in agreement.

Mitsuko steps in and decides to set the wedding date. "I think April of next year would be an auspicious time. It will be beautiful with the cherry blossoms in bloom. What do you think, Shina-sama? Would you rather choose another time?"

Shina looks at Masako and says, "What do you and Masahiro think? Is April of next year a good date? Perhaps you and Masahiro should take a stroll in the garden and discuss the matter. Please come back in thirty minutes. We have to settle the wedding plans and go home before it gets too late."

Masahiro takes Masako's hand and strolls along the garden path. They make small talk as they look at one other in lingering glances. They have so much to say but so little time. They decide to be agreeable with the April date and return to their waiting parents.

The two families agree to meet in a month to plan the wedding festivities. Masahiro and Masako beam in happiness. Fall is almost gone, and winter is approaching. Soon there will be snow on the mountain, and the two may not be able to meet in the icy weather.

In November, the parents meet and settle the wedding day, and the date is April 15, 1656. Masahiro will be seventeen and Masako sixteen. Matsue will make Masako's wedding kimono, and Mitsuko says she wants to pay for the wedding dress as a gift for Masako. Mitsuko orders the silk for the kimono from China and gives it to Matsue to sew. Shina says she wants to embroider the obi herself and begins to embroider gold and silver threads onto white obi silk. The wedding will bring guests from far and wide and will be the wedding of the century.

Masahiro tells Masako, "Love is like the wind. We can't see it, but we can feel it. I love you with all my heart and soul. I will love you forever."

Masako is touched—tears begin to flow—as she embraces Masahiro.

CHAPTER 13

Snow is falling, and the temperature drops to the low teens—at times to single digits. The cold front is not abating. The mountain is frozen, and no one can climb up or down. Masahiro paces the outside corridors of his home as he worries about Masako's safety.

Masako is huddling in front of their fireplace, and icicles are hanging from the rafters. Her father has piled up wood—enough to last for a few days. There is a foot of snow outside, and Shina is busy sewing Masako's obi. Shina gets up to stir the soup in the iron pot, and Kiyoko is writing a poem into a book. Everyone eats dinner and goes to bed.

Taiji attaches a rope running from the front door to the outbuilding. With the blizzard outside, he is worried one of his family may get lost while going to the privy.

Kiyoko pokes Masako and asks her to come with her to the outhouse. Masako ignores her and pretends to be asleep. Kiyoko gives up and puts on a coat and ventures outside. The snow is coming down so heavy she can barely see. Kiyoko grabs the rope and walks to the outbuilding. Her feet sink into the snow-covered ground, and she begins to slip and slide. Kiyoko finally makes it to the outhouse and enters. She can hear the wind howl as she comes back outside, and the flakes are so huge it looks like a blanket. Kiyoko grabs the rope and begins to return to the house. All of a sudden, the rope snaps and drops. Kiyoko starts to panic as her hand's search for the torn twine—it is impossible. The rope has come apart due to the freezing temperature, and Kiyoko can no longer see in front of her. Kiyoko goes back to the privy and decides to wait inside.

In the early morning, the snow is still coming down, and it is a cold and depressing day. Masako decides to go to the betto. She struggles in the deep snow as she looks for the half-buried building. Masako sweeps away the snow from the doorway before entering. She is surprised to see her sister inside.

"Kiyoko, what are you doing here? Are you asleep?"

There is no answer. Masako goes over to Kiyoko and shakes her—Kiyoko topples over. Masako lets out a scream and runs out, calling for her mother.

"Oka-san, come quickly. Kiyoko is in the betto, and I can't wake her up. I touched her, but she is so cold. Please hurry."

Kiyoko is dead and frozen from the cold temperature. Taiji finds the broken rope and begins to weep. He did not know a twine could freeze and snap, and Taiji blames himself for her death, and cannot be comforted. Masako recalls Kiyoko was trying to wake her up to go to the toilet, and she pretended to be asleep. Masako blames herself for the death of her sister. Shina is inconsolable. They wrap

Kiyoko's body into a silk shroud and lay her outside to keep her from decaying. They will take Kiyoko to the temple as soon as the weather breaks. Kiyoko will be cremated and buried.

The cold snap finally comes to an end after ten days, and Taiji puts Kiyoko's wrapped body onto his horse. The family bundles up and walks down to the village. The family cremates Kiyoko and Masahiro and his family join them for a short Buddhist service. The two families have tea, and they bury Kiyoko in the cemetery.

The New Year of 1656 arrives, and Masako's family is still in mourning. Shina is not up to making any feast for New Year's Day and is disheartened. Kiyoko's death has the entire family devastated. Mitsuko and Sange invite Masako's family for the New Year's Day feast. They send their regrets.

CHAPTER 14

Two riders arrive in Uji. The noble wears a brilliant blue and white silk kimono, and he wears a cape to counter the chilly weather and has a sword hanging by his side. The bodyguard has on a brown kimono and a haori jacket, and he has a yumi or a bow hanging from his saddle, and arrows are in a basket ready to be plucked. The people of the village open the way as the two men come into the marketplace. Everyone is in awe and wonders who this person of importance can be?

The noble's hair is a chonmage, and he shaves his pate, and the rest of his hair is in a bun. The bodyguard's hair is around nine inches long, and it is scooped back into a knot in the back of his head and tied together with a black ribbon band.

The two men halt, and the bodyguard steps down from his horse. He goes to a stall and asks where he can find Lord Sange of the Ouchi Clan. The stallkeeper bows and points in the direction of a gated house in the distance. The bodyguard leads his master to Lord Sange's house, raps on the gated door, and a guard peeks out and asks for them to identify themselves.

"I am Koji, and my master is Prince Takashige. We have come to meet with Lord Sange. Is the lord home?"

The guard opens the gate and calls out to a lad named Koichi.

"Koichi, go and ask Lord Sange to come to the front gate." The guard tells Koichi not to tarry.

"Lord Sange, Lord Sange. Guard Toshio wants you to come to the front gate. He says it is crucial and asks you to hurry."

"Koichi, what is it? Stop shouting and calm down. Who is at the gate?"

Koichi bows and says, "I don't know, but Guard Toshio said an important person, is outside, and you need to come at once."

Sange puts on his footwear and hurries towards the front gate—trying to see who is outside. Sange steps forward and is shocked to see a Royal on his horse. Sange bows in deference to the high-ranking personage.

"*Dōzo oagatte kudasai mase,* please come to my house. I am Lord Sange of the Ouchi Clan. How may I be of service?"

"I am Prince Takashige, and I believe you are acquainted with my father, Lord Kanaage?"

The prince hands his bodyguard the reins to his horse and enters the gate. Sange is bowing lower.

"It is an honour to have you visit my home. Yes, I know your father very well, and he is a good friend. Please come in, and I will have sake brought in immediately."

The prince enters the tatami room overlooking the beautiful Japanese garden. The February air is cold, and Lord Sange closes the open shoji door. He calls for a maid.

"Nori, bring some sake immediately. Would you like some dinner? Your man can eat in the kitchen."

"Koji will eat with me, and he is not my servant. He is a very loyal and trusted friend."

"I apologize for my rudeness, and of course, your friend can eat with you. I will have your horses fed and watered in my stables."

Prince Takashige and Koji enjoy a scrumptious meal. Lord Sange asks if they will like to stay the night, and he will have Nori prepare a room.

"*Domo arigato gozaimasu,* thank you very much. We would like to spend a few days in your company if it isn't too much bother. We are a long way from home, and we are trying to find someone. It has come to my attention that the woman I seek may be residing here in Uji."

"I know most of the women from samurai families in this village. Tell me her name and I can tell you if I know her. Does she belong to the Ouchi Clan?"

I think she is in hiding and using an alias. The girl is sixteen years of age, and she is my second cousin. I was betrothed to her when she born. Unfortunately, my uncle, Emperor Morihito, was killed, and my aunt, Empress Kanaye, died at childbirth. My betrothed's name is Princess Akiko."

Sange almost chokes on his sake when he hears Princess Akiko's name. He recovers and tells the prince he does not know of anyone named Akiko in the village of Uji. He is not lying—Masako lives on the mountain.

Prince Takeshige and his bodyguard take a bath and retire for the night. Sange goes in search of his father and his wife. Mitsuko is reading in their bedchamber. Sange asks Nori to have his father come to their room at once. Mitsuko looks at her husband's face and knows something is amiss.

Mito knocks on the door and says, "What is it now? I had a wonderful dream. I was by the ocean, and a white heron was walking on the beach. Suddenly the heron turned into a beautiful young maiden, and I was having my way with her when I was rudely interrupted."

Mitsuko laughs and says, "You wish you are twenty again. Sorry, your dream disappeared with one knock of your bedchamber door. Come in, and I will have some tea brought in."

Sange puts his finger to his mouth to signify silence and whispers, "I have some terrible news. Prince Takeshige is in the guest room with his bodyguard Koji, and they are here to find Princess Akiko. The prince claims he and the princess were to be married when the princess was born. Prince Takeshige heard the princess lives in Uji under an assumed name. I told him no one named Akiko lives in this village. I did not tell a lie since Masako lives up on the mountain. What should we do? Maybe we should warn Shina and Taiji. Should we tell Masahiro? Oh, what a mess!"

Mitsuko begins to wring her hands, and Mito has a frown on his face. Sange looks from one face to another and heaves a big sigh. This situation is a disaster. Sange calls for Nori and asks her to bring Masahiro at once.

Masahiro is yawning as he steps into his parent's bedchamber.

"Is something wrong? Why did you summon me when I was already asleep?"

Mitsuko relays the story to her son, and Masahiro is suddenly wide-awake.

"What are we going to do? I can't give up, Masako. Father give me some coins so I can take Masako away—I need to pack," Masahiro says as he rushes from the room.

Mitsuko is running to catch Masahiro. She needs to calm her son. The prince does not know the true identity of the princess, and he may never find out.

Only seven people know about Masako, and the seven will never give out their secret. Tomorrow she will send Masahiro up the mountain to tell Masako's family to keep a low profile and not come down to the village. Mitsuko hands Masahiro some coins to use in case he has to flee.

Mitsuko greets her guests at breakfast, and she is gracious and remains calm. Mitsuko pretends not to know Princess Akiko and withdraws when her husband appears. Sange walks in nervously and puts on a smile and tries to appear nonchalant.

Masahiro leaves for the mountain to warn Masako and her family. Masako is surprised when Masahiro arrives.

Masako says, "I'm happy to see you, but what are you doing here, Masahiro? I didn't know you were coming, and you look worried. Did something bad happen to your family? Tell me what's going on."

Masahiro explains that Prince Takeshige is staying at his home. According to the prince, he and Princess Akiko were to be married at birth. Someone told

Prince Takeshige that Princess Akiko lived in Uji under an assumed name, and he came to find the princess.

"We told the prince that we do not know anyone living in Uji named Akiko. That was the truth, and we did not lie. I don't know how long it will be before he discovers that you are Princess Akiko. My parents sent me here to warn you, and I think it would be best if you and I get married immediately. We can be married in another village far away. If the prince finds out you are Princess Akiko, my family can pretend we didn't know. By that time, he will be unable to do anything. What do you think?"

Shina replies, "Prince Takeshige most likely will not be able to recognize Taiji or me. It has been sixteen years since we were in the palace, and he would have only been a young boy of one. I don't know how he is going to recognize Princess Akiko even if he sees her. Did he have something he could use to identify her?"

"Masako-sama, do you have any identifying marks on your body? It could be a small mole or a birthmark. If the prince knows about one of these marks, he may be able to put two and two together. Shina-sama, did you ever see something like that when you used to bathe Masako when she was a baby?"

"Masako does have a blue birthmark in the shape of a heart on her buttocks. Most Japanese babies have blue birthmarks on their bodies, but perhaps none in the shape of a heart. I don't know if it is still there? Masako, let us go into the bedroom so I can check."

Shina and Masako disappear into the bedroom. Masako undresses, and her mother brings a lantern to see if the birthmark is still visible.

Shina gasps and says, "It is still there, and I don't know if the prince knows about the mark. The only person that might know is the midwife that delivered you. The midwife will be in her late seventies if she is still living. Also, the prince can hardly undress you to look for the birthmark. I don't think we have to worry if we all keep our secret."

"I still think Masako-san and I should get married as soon as possible. I am willing to run away. What do you think, Masako?"

"Masahiro, if you think getting married as soon as possible would be the best, I will do as you say. We can leave early tomorrow for Mt Koyasan. One of the monks can perform the ceremony, and we can stay there for a week. It will be sad not to have our families there, but time is crucial. My wedding kimono is still not done, but I can save it for one of our daughters if we are lucky to have one in the future."

Shina and Taiji begin to help their daughter pack. Since Masahiro did not bring any clothes, he borrows some from Taiji. Masahiro's kimono is too costly, and Taiji thinks his clothes would be less noticeable. Taiji tells Masahiro to change his clothes, and the less conspicuous the couple looks, the better.

Masahiro has not told his parents about his marriage plans, and he worries they will be angry when they find out. Masahiro tells Masako it is somewhat of an emergency. No one can inform his parents of the pending marriage because the prince is staying at his home and may overhear. Masahiro worries that his parents will wonder what happened to him when he does not come home. Taiji says he will try to get a message to his father or mother as soon as possible.

In the early dawn, Masahiro and Masako get ready to leave for Mt. Koya. Masako's mother hands Masahiro a few bronze coins. Shina decides she will only give Masahiro one gold coin for an emergency. Shina tells Masahiro not to use the gold coin unless necessary.

Shina makes an obento with rice balls, fried chicken, and rice cakes for dessert. Masako and Masahiro's clothing are inside a nondescript brown gunnysack, and they are traveling as though they are just an ordinary couple on their way to be married. Taiji takes the couple up the snowy path in a wooden cart pulled by two horses. Taiji takes Masako and

Masahiro as close as he dares to the monastery and returns home.

Masahiro throws the gunnysack over his right shoulder and onto his back. They see candle-lit buildings as they approach the monastery. Masahiro is familiar with the grounds since he was here a few months past with his father.

The couple approach a monk dressed in a blue robe with a conical hat who is sweeping the entry to the monastery. Masahiro inquires whom they should see to be married. The monk says he will take them to Abbot Monji, the chief monk of the temple, and leads them to a small plain at the top of Mt. Koya. It is a sacred area known as the Danjo Garan. The abbot is sitting in front of a Buddhist altar, chanting, and praying. The abbot has on a saffron-coloured robe, and his head shaved. He has wooden beads between his clasped hands while bowing. The monk tells Masahiro and Masako to wait until the abbot is through with his ritual.

An hour later, the abbot rises and seems to be startled to see strangers in the temple. He smiles and gestures for them to come forward and asks what he can do for them. Masahiro says he and Masako would like to get married as soon as possible. The abbot asks why they are in such a hurry. Masahiro says they must return to their home before they become snowbound.

"Do your parents know you are here? Is there any objection from them for you to wed? What are your names? I am Abbot Monji."

"My name is Masahiro, and this is Masako. Our parents are happy that we are marrying, but they were unable to come today because of the bad weather. We were supposed to get married in the spring, but Masako and I can no longer wait. We want to be married before the baby comes, and it would be an embarrassment to be unwed."

The abbot looks towards Masako with his piercing eyes. He asks Masako if she too would like to marry as soon as possible. Masako says, yes, and shyly looks away.

"We will have the ceremony tomorrow morning at eight. In the meantime, you may remain in one of the rooms here at the temple. You can join us in having a light breakfast at six. Unfortunately, the bathhouse is off-limits to any woman, so a bowl of warm water, soap and a cloth will be brought for you to wash."

The abbot tells Masahiro he is welcome to come to the ofuro or bath before going to bed. Masako and Masahiro thank the abbot and bow as he departs.

A monk appears with a bowl of warm water, soap, and a towel. He leads the couple to a small room with a futon and two pillows and bows goodnight. Masahiro tells Masako he will go to take a bath and be right back. Masako hurriedly washes up and takes off her kimono and changes into blue and white yukata nightwear. Masako dives under the futon and begins to tremble as she waits for Masahiro's return.

Masahiro takes his time in the bath. He knows Masako is feeling apprehensive about sleeping in the same room. He hopes by the time he returns; she will be fast asleep.

An hour later, Masahiro returns from the bathhouse and slides open the shoji door and glances at Masako to see if she is asleep. Masahiro notices she is still awake, and her body is shaking, and her eyelids are twitching. He lies down beside her and pulls the futon over his body. Masahiro blows out the lantern, and the room suddenly becomes dark, and he turns away from Masako and pretends to sleep. Masahiro can hear a sigh of relief coming from Masako as she relaxes.

The wedding ceremony is lengthy, and there is a great deal of praying and incense burning. Ten monks have joined in the celebration, and they are chanting. The abbot takes a cup of sake and offers it to Masahiro. Masahiro takes a sip, and the abbot turns to Masako and offers her the rice wine, and Masako takes a small sip, and the wedding is over. Everyone congratulates the happy couple, and they return to their room to change from their wedding clothes to more comfortable attire. Masako and Masahiro decide to tour the grounds of the monastery. Snow is still falling, and the temperature is dropping. In the late afternoon, the snowfall becomes a blinding blizzard, and they become snowbound. Lunch is brought to their room by two monks carrying a tray with bowls of miso soup, cold tofu with sauce, pickled vegetables, and brown bran rice. Although the monks are vegetarians, the food proves to be delicious.

Masako is sipping green tea and nervously looking away from her husband. Masahiro knows he must take it slow and easy, so he doesn't frighten his new bride. Masahiro looks down at Masako, and she sees a longing in his eyes.

"Masako, I want to make love to you now. Are you ready? Please do not worry and try to relax and enjoy the lovemaking. I will go slow and make this first time as pleasurable as possible. You will feel a sharp pain when I pierce your maidenhead, and after that, you should only feel pleasure. Let me undress you."

Masako replies, "Thank you for being such a considerate husband. I don't know anything about the marriage bed, and my mother was going to tell me before our marriage in the spring, but she didn't have time when we decided to elope. Please show me what I'm supposed to do to please you, and I hope I am not inadequate, and you don't find me an apt lover."

Masahiro begins to undress Masako, and she tries to look away, but Masahiro tells her to look at him. After Masako is entirely nude, Masahiro cannot take his eyes off of Masako's beautiful black hair covering her breasts. Masahiro begins to stroke her breasts and pinches her pebbled nipples. Masako moans, and her mouth gapes open. Masahiro pauses to undress, and Masako looks down onto his manhood and gasps.

"Masako, you have seen horses, mate, haven't you? The horse mating is similar to our lovemaking, but our lovemaking is much more satisfying. Their lovemaking only lasts for a moment or two, but ours will go on and on. I promise you will grow to enjoy it and someday we will make a family. Please let me love you," whispers Masahiro.

Masahiro begins to fondle Masako's breasts, and Masako's head falls back. His bride's body twitches as he applies pressure and begins to rotate his fingers.

Masako lets out a groan and grabs her husband around the neck. Masahiro reaches Masako's maidenhead, pauses, and wants to get it over as fast as he can—and he abruptly pushes forward. He hears Masako call out in pain, and he stops. He looks into her troubled eyes and tells her the pain is over. He slowly begins to move in and out, and Masako relaxes. She suddenly stiffens, and a low moan comes from her throat as wave after wave of pleasure washes over her. Masahiro hastens his motions, and his desire spirals upwards, erupting in a shuddering convulsive release. He holds himself above her as the tensions in his muscles abate. Masahiro eases down beside Masako and pulls her against his side—cradling her head.

"Masako, are you all right? I hope I didn't hurt you too badly, and I tried to be as gentle as possible. I'm sorry, but every woman must go through the pain the first time."

Masako says, "Thank you, it was wonderful. The pain was sudden, but it diminished almost immediately. It was the most thrilling moment of my life. I felt like I was floating up to heaven and never wanted to come back down. Can we try it again?"

Masahiro begins to laugh. He tells Masako he needs a little break before he can continue. He tells her that men are not like women. Women can go on and on without rest, but a man must recuperate before doing the act again.

Masako asks, "how long do you need?"

Masahiro feels a stirring, and he says, "I think I have rested enough."

Masahiro and Masako snuggle together through the night, and they wake up and make love two more times. Masako feels sore but is content and enjoys the lovemaking. Drowsiness and contentment make her eyes droop shut as she drifts asleep. When Masako awakens in the morning, she notices bloodstains on the futon. Masako goes to the bowl of water and scrubs the blood from the quilt.

It is time to return home, and Masako gathers up their clothes and begins to pack. Masako goes to the kitchen and asks if they could make a small obento and gives them a coin. Masahiro returns from a stroll and says he has procured a short ride. The farmer can take them halfway down the mountain, and they will have to walk the rest of the way.

It is almost midnight when the newlyweds spot Masako's house, and they are lucky no new snow has fallen. It is a cold crisp night with stars shining through the thick trees of the snow-covered forest. Masahiro and Masako quicken their steps.

Suddenly, a lantern shines in the dark, and Taiji is standing with a sword. Taiji is relieved to see Masako and extends his arms as she runs into them. Shina looks shaken as she comes into the lit room. A smile crosses Shina's face as she sees her daughter and her new husband.

"Welcome home, and congratulations, you are now husband and wife. Everything is calm, and no bad news has come from your parents. We have not gone down to the village and have stayed away. We don't want to raise any suspicions and hope the prince has gone home. Masahiro, do you want to go home to see your family? I think it would be best if Masako remains here."

The following afternoon Masahiro returns home. His mother greets him warmly.

"Masako's father sent a message that you were going to be married. Prince Takeshige is still here, and his bodyguard is going from door to door in search of Princess Akiko. The villagers do not know anything about the princess, and the prince is becoming frustrated. Prince Takeshige may soon go to neighboring villages and even up the mountain in search. We must keep our voices down so the prince cannot hear our words."

"Oka-san, Masako, and I got married a week ago. We went up to Mt Koyasan and had a Buddhist ceremony, and Abbot Monji and ten of his monks performed the wedding rites. Masako and I have consummated our marriage, and no one can dissolve our union. I married a woman named Masako and know nothing about a royal named Princess Akiko. I don't think the prince will want Masako when he finds out she is no longer a virgin."

"Masahiro, what are you going to do? Are you going to live on the mountain with Masako's family until the prince leaves? It would seem suspicious if you left today without meeting the prince and his bodyguard—I think you should stay for dinner."

Prince Takeshige is cordial and pleased to meet Masahiro. The prince asks Masahiro if he is married and has children. Masahiro says he is married and looking forward to the day his wife presents him with a son or daughter.

"How long have you been married, and where is your wife? I would like to meet her if I may. I'm sure she must be a beauty, and you have hidden her away," laughs the prince jokingly.

"Masako is away visiting with her family, and if you are still here when she gets back, I will gladly introduce you. Masako's sister recently died, and the family is still in mourning."

"You say your wife's sister passed away? What was her name, and how old was she? She may be Princess Akiko that I am seeking," explains the prince excitedly.

"I know nothing about Masako's sister being a princess. That is absurd! All I know is Kiyoko was adopted when she was a newborn."

Mitsuko is listening as Masahiro weaves his little lie. She is pleased that this tale might just appease the prince. If the prince believes the princess is dead, he will leave and not return. Mitsuko excuses herself and sends a message to Shina and Taiji.

Taiji receives the letter from Masahiro's mother, and he calls Shina and Masako to read the note together. Mitsuko says if the prince believes Kiyoko is Princess Akiko, and she is dead, he will be satisfied with the tale and leave. If the prince contacts them, Mitsuko would like Shina and Taiji to verify Kiyoko's adoption and death. Mitsuko believes this little tale will be a solution to Masako and Masahiro's problem.

"Oka-san, will you tell the prince this little lie so Masahiro and I can live a good life? I know you don't like to be dishonest, but this would be the perfect answer to our problem. Please, if you do this for me, I will be grateful to you for the rest of my life," pleads Masako.

Shina nods her head and says she will go along with this tale. Kiyoko is dead, and she will not be coming back. Kiyoko would be pleased to help her sister even from her grave. Tears are streaming down Shina's face as she hugs Masako.

The next day, there is a knock at the door, and Shina sees Prince Takeshige standing at her doorstep.

"*Ohayo-gozaimasu*, good morning. What can I do for you? My name is Shina, and I live here with my husband, Taiji. He is down at the village today and will be home soon."

"Thank you for receiving me so graciously. I am Prince Takeshige, and I am looking for a young girl that maybe my second cousin, Princess Akiko. I heard one of your daughters recently passed away, and she was sixteen? I am sorry to bother you at this time, but I need to find out if she was Princess Akiko. Do you know anything about this matter?"

Shina tries to look surprised. She begins to stutter and look nervously around. The prince sees she is agitated and tries to calm her down.

"I did not want to upset you. I only want to find the princess. Can you help me?"

"Since my daughter is already dead, I guess it doesn't matter if you know her true identity. Yes, my daughter was Princess Akiko. My husband was the Captain of the Guards, and I was a Lady in Waiting for the empress. When the emperor was injured and lay dying, he ordered us to take the baby and flee. Taiji and I have lived here on the mountain for more than eighteen years. I will show you the royal kimono that Princess Akiko was wearing after she was born. I also have a gold bracelet. Would you like to see them?"

"Yes, I would, if it isn't too much bother. The kimono and bracelet will be the evidence I need to halt any further searches. You may keep the mementos—I only need to see them. *Domo arigato gozaimasu*—thank you very much. I appreciate you raising the princess and everything you have done for her before her death. I would like to visit her gravesite and pray."

Shina brings the royal kimono and the gold bracelet for the prince to see. He has tears in his eyes as he strokes them. Shina draws a map for Princess Akiko's gravesite, and the prince thanks her for her help and departs.

Masako runs into the room and hugs her mother. She is thankful for the little lie her mother has told the prince. She wants to go down into the village to tell her husband, but she stops herself. She realizes she needs to wait a few days until the prince is gone.

In the next few days, the cold front is back. There is a daily snowfall that brings down an inch one day and five inches the next. The bitter cold lingers while the temperature drops to single digits. Masako cannot go to the village, and Masahiro cannot climb the mountain. The snow muffles all sound, and there is nothing but silence.

A rumbling noise awakens Masako, and she races to the window and watches as the mountain comes down. It is an avalanche. Before she can open the front door, the snow covers the house. Her father and mother come out of their room, looking horrified. The rumbling sound is slowly fading. Taiji says they must dig out as soon as possible before their oxygen supply diminishes. Taiji carefully opens the front door, and snow comes plunging into the house.

Taiji decides to feed the fireplace with more logs. He thinks perhaps the heat from the chimney may melt some of the snow, and they may be able to get some air. He hopes the chimney is still above the snowline and not buried. Taiji is mistaken, and the snow-plugged chimney makes the smoke pour back into the house. Taiji again opens the front door and begins to tunnel out. He hears shouting and scraping—someone is trying to dig them out.

Masahiro has arrived after the avalanche, and he can barely see the house under the snow. He finds a stick, and frantically begins to dig. He yells out to Masako and says he is trying to rescue them. Inside it is getting harder to breathe.

Masako hears a barking of a dog and wonders if the dog belongs to Masahiro. She follows her father into the tunnel and helps him dig. Her hands are so cold they are turning numb, and Shina has found some wooden spoons to help. Suddenly another rumble is heard, and more snow comes down. This time they are lucky, and the avalanche clears off some of the snow in front of their house. Taiji has found an opening and stands to gulp the fresh cold air. Masako and Shina feel the stiff breeze coming down the shaft and sigh in relief. Suddenly a dog comes bounding down the tunnel with Masahiro trailing behind. The dog jumps on Masako and knocks her down. Masahiro laughs and says the dog does not belong to him.

Taiji is worried about his neighbors and goes to see if the avalanche has done damage to their homes. Taiji prays the snow has not buried his friends. He finds Saburo coming through a small opening, and Saburo says Kenji and Matsue are not home. They have gone to the village to stay with the village smith until winter is over.

Masahiro says, "I have come to tell you Prince Takeshige has left. He went to pay respects to Kiyoko's gravesite, and he is satisfied that Princess Akiko is dead. We have nothing more to fear, and we can go on with our married life. Masako, will you come down from the mountain and come live with me in Uji?"

Shina and Taiji want her to stay, but they know that is impossible. Masako deserves a better life. They help her pack her belongings.

"I will visit you often. I love you both and want to thank you for taking care of me all these years. *Domo arigato gozaimashita,* thank you," bows Masako to her parents. Happy tears are flowing as they hug goodbye.

CHAPTER 15

Three years fly by, and it is 1659, and Masahiro and Masako have three children. The oldest child is a boy called Yoshiaki. The twins are a boy and a girl, and their names are Kazuo and Midori. The boys are handsome like their father, and Midori is a beauty like her mother.

Grandfather Mito falls ill and becomes bedridden, and he has gout in his right toe, and his arthritic fingers are bent. Mito had fallen the previous winter and never recovered. The doctor had to amputate Mito's left leg due to diabetes, and the doctors gave up hope of his recovery and said he only has a few months to live. He loves his great-grandchildren, and they often play in his bedchamber. He never tires looking at them, and their noisy play never bothers him. Although he is in deep pain, he smiles and pretends all is well.

Mito moves his bedchamber closer to the privy. He is pale with fever and feels chilled. His daughter-in-law has sewn him a quilted vest to wear over his yukata. Mito asks for a sip of sake, and Mitsuko orders the maid to bring it immediately.

Mito finishes his supper, and a maid bathes him before putting him to bed. He wears diapers now, but he never shows his shame. He is a model patient, and the family treats him like he is normal. Mito dreams about his younger days when he had just become a samurai warrior. Memories come flooding back.

Mito was seventeen when his father died, and his mother died the following year. He was from a family of generations of samurai warriors. Mito was quick of wit and excelled in all the skills needed to be a great warrior. His swordsmanship known throughout Japan, Mito, was the envy of the upcoming young samurai warriors of the Ouchi Clan. The other samurai clans feared Mito's sword.

Mito married a beautiful maiden named Chikari. She was from another samurai family located in eastern Japan. It was not a love match, but an arranged marriage. In the end, they grew to love one another, and their short marriage was happy. They had one son and named him Sange. Chikari died giving birth to Sange, and Mito never got over his loss. Mito never remarried, although many samurai clans would have welcomed him as their son-in-law.

The August sun was sweltering, and it was two years since Chikari's death. Mito was dressed all in black with his topknot tied with a black ribbon. He was unshaven and seemed not to care about his looks. Mito was despondent, and he knew he had to snap out of his sorrow for his son's sake.

The air was stifling, and Mito's perspiration rolled down his neck and back. For the past few years, the upper-samurai dominated over the lower-samurai. Mito had watched a lower-samurai commit suicide. The man had gotten drunk to cover up his fear of taking his own life. He had sliced open his stomach below his navel in a horizontal direction. He then pierced the right side of his throat, slashing across to the left side of his neck. Blood gushed out of his wound. The samurai had run away from a battle and was marked a coward. A few hours later, his wife and two children were found dead. The wife and children had committed seppuku. They were obligated to follow him in death to recover honour for their family.

Mito was an expert swordsman. He could chop bundles of straw with his sword, return his sword with his right hand to his scabbard before the cut straw hit the floor. The lower-samurai watched in awe as Mito used his sword in a flash of an eye.

Heavy rain was falling, the hour was late, and Mito held an umbrella against the pouring rain. It was dark, with no lanterns lit as he walked. All of a sudden, two sword-wielding samurai appeared. One of the attackers let out a bloodcurdling wail as he brought his blade downwards. Mito deflected the attack with his bamboo umbrella. He received a wound on his shoulder that drew blood. The blood was spraying, and his kimono was bloody. Mito reached for his sword and quickly drew his blade. Mito cut down his attackers on the spot. He could not identify the clan. Mito guessed they were two rogue warriors on their own.

It was another rainy night as Mito walked down the street. A young courtesan was walking a few feet ahead. She had on a colorful blue kimono with peonies at the hemline. Suddenly six swordsmen appeared and surrounded her. Mito drew his sword and struck. He told the young courtesan to stay behind him as he circled the attackers. Mito sliced into one man and then another. As he chased the third man, he sliced him through his neck, and the other three men fled.

Mito proudly watched his son grow into a handsome man. Sange's swordsmanship was equal to his own. Sange wrote sonnets and painted beautiful scenes of nature, and he was quick and excelled in planning battle strategies. By the time Sange was seventeen, most men had spoken his name in awe.

Mito remembered the yearly trip to Mt. Koyasan with Sange. It was a time when a father and son bond. Now Sange was making the arduous trip with his son Masahiro. Mito was too old and sick to travel.

Sange had married a beautiful woman named Mitsuko, and she was from a prestigious samurai family. This relationship was a love match, and happiness radiated from their souls. When his grandson was born, he was a very proud grandfather. Masahiro grew to be an excellent swordsman, poet, and code breaker. Mito was proud when Masahiro married a charming girl named Masako. There were family secrets that had to be hush-hush, but overall, life was good.

A lifetime ago, Mito remembered being on a ship, and he had never been so scared. Giant waves were crashing against the hull, and the wind was howling as the seawater slid across the slippery deck. He had tied himself to a pole and prayed the storm would go away. The ship continued in a sideways motion and spray after spray of water hit his face as he turned away. Mito could hear the shouts of the ship's crew as they tried to take control. Mito heard a loud crack over his head, and as he looked up, the mast came crashing down. When Mito woke, he was in a small harbor in calm waters. That was the last time he ventured out to sea.

Mito tires as he lies in bed, and his aches and pains are constant. He closes his eyes and tries to sleep. Suddenly, at midnight his eyes fly open. Mito finds himself in the cemetery. He blinks and sees his dead wife Chikari smile as she draws near. Mito doesn't know if he is awake or dreaming. Memories begin to fade, and he is now in the present.

"Mito, I have come to escort you to the land of the Buddha. Are you ready? I have waited for you for a very long time. I have missed you, and now we can be together forever. Take my hand, and we can walk into the white light."

Surrounded by the animated faces from the past, Mito is full of happiness. The air is calming and refreshing, and Mito no longer feels any pain. He takes Chikari's hand and walks into the blinding light. He feels a lightness he has never experienced. Mito looks at his wife, and she looks as though she has never aged. She is again a maiden, and he is a young man.

The next morning Sange finds his father dead, and his face looks peaceful and serene. Tears flow from Sange's eyes as he lovingly touches his father's wrinkled hand. Sange calls out to Mitsuko and the grandchildren to tell them of Mito's death. They come running as more tears flow.

"Death is always a reason for sadness, but life goes on. Our family will survive," says Sange sadly.

Mito is cremated and buried in their family plot with a large stone carved with Mito's name, date of birth, and date of death. He was a beloved member of the Ouchi Clan, and many come to pay their respect.

Other samurai clansmen also come in groves. It is a large gathering to honour a great man.

Masahiro's sister Miho is devastated that her grandfather is dead. She is not a beauty like her mother, Mitsuko, but she has an endearing quality. She is quiet and agreeable. Her one desire is to become a nun. She goes to the nearby Buddhist temple to pray once a month. Miho spends a great deal of her spare time in meditation in the forests around the lake close to home. Miho has kept all her activities a secret from her family. She knows they will be in shock if she ever reveals her goal in life.

Miho finally takes her vows and dons a purple robe and shaves off her hair. She is sitting at home, waiting for her family to appear for breakfast. The servants had already had a shock when they realized the nun was Miho. They are whispering and staring.

Shiso is the first to arrive and sees a Buddhist nun eating breakfast. He does not recognize that it is his younger sister.

"*Ohayo gozaimasu.* Good morning. Do my parents know you are here? I will ask the maid to summon them. Nori, please tell my mother and father to come. We have a visitor."

Miho speaks up, "Shiso; it is I Miho. Do you not know your sister?"

"What are you saying? My sister is probably still in bed. She is always the last one to rise."

Mitsuko and Sange come rushing in. They see the nun and bow.

"Welcome, have you come to pray for my father's soul?" questions Sange.

"Father, don't you recognize me? It's me, Miho. I have come to tell you I have become a Buddhist nun and will be leaving this house today forever. I wanted to thank you and mother for raising me with love and devotion all these many years. I will be staying at the Gichi Temple about ten miles away. I can come to visit once a year but other than that I cannot come home. I will be studying the Buddha's teachings and offering my services to the poor and suffering. I will remain celibate for the remainder of my life. I must focus fulltime on transforming my mind and heart for the good of humankind. I will be living a simple and disciplined life. I do not need any more clothing other than this robe. I have shaved my head to let go of all vanity and worldly attachments. I am deeply sorry if I have shocked you. I pray you can accept my new life. My life as a nun is what I desire, and I hope you can forgive me."

Sange and Mitsuko are in shock. Shiso begins to berate Miho, but Sange tells him to stop. He looks at his daughter and shakes his head in disbelief. Mitsuko starts to sob, and her shoulders shake. Suddenly, Mitsuko rises and races from the room in unbearable sorrow. Sange tells Shiso to look after his mother, and Sange says he wishes to speak to Miho alone.

"Miho, why did you not tell us? You probably thought we would stop you, and you would not be able to follow your heart. You are probably right, but if this is the life you choose, I will support you."

"Thank you, Father. It is such a relief to hear you say you are on my side. I hope Shiso and mother eventually will feel the same. I am sorry I have shocked everyone. I am going to leave now before anyone confronts me with ill feelings. I will be coming to the village to help build an orphanage, and I pray that both you and my mother can understand my heart and forgive me. I will drop by in the next few weeks when I return. Perhaps you can contribute towards the orphanage with some rice and supplies?"

Miho bows ten times to her father as he stares. He has tears in his eyes as he realizes he has lost his daughter forever. Sange hopes she is going to be happy with her choice of life. He will support her as much as possible.

"I will speak to your mother and brother, and I also need to tell Masahiro and Masako. Your mother is hurt right now, but she will eventually understand. Shiso is in shock and will also come around. You are always welcome in this house. Never forget that! I will take you back to the temple to see the place you have chosen to live. You will always be my daughter as long as I live. I will send some of my soldiers to help with the construction of the orphanage, and I will supply them with rice and blankets. Let me know if there is anything else you need, and please do not hesitate to ask. Let's go now before it becomes too late."

Miho follows her father out to the palanquin. She bows to all the servants. They bow back with surprised looks on their faces. Some of the elderly maids have tears streaming down their cheeks. They have watched Miho go from a wee baby to a young woman. They wish her well but cannot understand how someone that has all her wealth wants to become a poor nun?

It is late afternoon when Miho and Sange arrive at the temple, and the head nun welcomes Sange. She is a woman in her middle years wearing a saffron-coloured robe. All the other nuns wear purple robes, and their hair shaved. She asks Sange to stay for tea. Sange asks to see where Miho will be sleeping. Men are forbidden to go into the nun's bedchambers. She assures Sange that Miho will be safe. She permits Miho to visit her family the following week. Sange says his goodbyes and leaves Miho standing outside with tears of happiness.

Mitsuko cannot sleep. Night after night, she tosses in her bed sobbing. She is like a ghost when she is awake. She walks around in unendurable sadness. She tries to understand Miho's determination to leave their family and enter a Buddhist temple. In her anguish, she decides to visit Miho's new home. The head nun explains that Miho has given up all worldly dreams and has sacrificed herself for the salvation of the poor and infirm.

"Your daughter believes in reincarnation. She says she has chosen this life to pay back the debt of her past transgressions in another life. She is very pure of heart, and you and your husband have raised her well. I will make sure she is safe and treat her like she is my daughter. I usually do not allow new nuns to visit their family, but I will let Miho stay with you a few days while she works at the new orphanage. I want to lessen your shock, and for the sake of your sanity, I will allow her this one favor. I hope you will not badger her and ask her to give up her new life. I hope you will be supportive so she can be happy in her transition into our Buddhist way of living. Please think deeply into your heart, and give up your fight to make her return home. You do want your daughter to be happy, don't you?"

Mitsuko is so frustrated she decides to give up and let her daughter choose her own life. When she lets out her anger, her depression dissipates. Mitsuko seeks out Sange and tells him her decision to let Miho be. He is so relieved he sends a message to Miho that her mother has finally relented.

The head nun has explained the process of reincarnation to Mitsuko. She says the Buddhists believe that desires cause suffering. In Buddhism, when one dies, either he or she attains liberation, or he or she comes back in another form through rebirth. This process takes forty-nine days, or it might be immediately after death. Buddhism teaches a person's soul is affected by the influences of karma. Karma refers to the spiritual principle of cause and effect. The way the person lives determines how and when they will eventually reach nirvana. The nun tells Mitsuko her daughter's goal is to reach the pure land as soon as possible.

Mitsuko is suddenly hungry. She has not eaten well since Miho had left to return to the temple. She asks Nori to bring some food and tea. She is so fatigued she lies down and closes her eyes. She is fast asleep when Nori returns with her tray. Nori covers Mitsuko with a futon and tiptoes out of the room.

Sange returns from a meeting with his clansmen. Nori tells him Mitsuko is sleeping and has not yet eaten. Sange tells Nori to bring in both their dinners to their bedchamber. He gently nudges Mitsuko until she opens her eyes.

"It is time for dinner. Nori will be bringing in our food in a few minutes. Did you have a nice rest? I have sent a message to Miho that you have decided to support her. I hope that is all right with you? I know Miho is going to be very happy with your generous support."

Miho finds out there is no distinction between her and the priests. They are considered equal. They are supposed to live a life that reflects the attitudes and values of a person or a group. She is not allowed to have personal means of support, and she will have to seek alms that make her contemplate and understand the things that are necessary for her life. She is going to dedicate her life to observing poverty, chastity, and obedience. Miho will live in a community focused on meditation, study, and prayers.

The head nun gives Miho her daily schedule, and Miho will meditate and pray every day. She will rise at four in the morning when the bell strikes. There will be sutra chanting at a quarter past five, and the head nun will interview Miho until she goes to breakfast at seven. Her breakfast consists of rice gruel, salted plum, and pickles. Between eight and almost eleven, she will clean and do menial duties. At eleven, she will partake of barley rice, miso soup, cooked vegetables, and pickled radish for lunch. At four in the afternoon, the nuns will eat a light meal similar to lunch. There is silence at every meal. There will be a variation on the type of vegetables served. Between five and eight-thirty, Miho will have to meditate and meet with the head nun. At nine in the evening, the lights have to go out, and from nine to eleven, they will sit and meditate. When not contemplating, Miho will engage in studying religious books, cleaning, gardening, farming, or go outside the temple to ask for alms. The days are full and no time for idle fingers.

Miho holds beads called nenju in her left hand, and the one hundred eight beads are made of sandalwood and have a subtle, pleasant scent. They use the beads in prayer, meditation, and chanting. In worship, the double loop of beads can be placed over the fingers of both hands, letting them rest between the fingers and the thumb, while bringing the hands together in gassho or prayer. The nuns always carry their beads wherever they go.

Miho decides to gift her family with prayer beads. The beads will only have twenty-seven beads instead of the formal one hundred and eight. She will give them the beads when she meets them the following week. The beads will be the final present she will be presenting. From now, on she will have to live in poverty and will have no money to spend. She may have to beg in the streets for alms.

The construction site is in full swing. Sange has sent twenty soldiers to help, and he is there himself to aid and direct. Miho finds him eating lunch with the construction workers. Mitsuko is standing in front of a long table, passing out food. Shiso is gone.

"Father, it is good to see you. Thank you for all the help. I am going to go and speak to mother."

"Mother, I hope you have forgiven me? I am sorry to have ruined your plans for my future. I am grateful to you and father, but I am going to serve my church and people. I am happy more than I can say. I know my life will not be easy, but this is how I want to spend the rest of my days. I hope you understand?" says Miho.

Mitsuko sighs as she listens to her daughter, and Miho professes her love for her religious life. Mitsuko has given up all hope for seeing her married into a samurai family with many children. Mitsuko has a broken heart, but she gives a smile in support.

"Miho, you know your father, and I wanted the best life for you? I am trying to understand, but it is very hard for me. You are giving up so much that other women would step into your shoes in a heartbeat. You are admirable, and I wish you the best. If ever you decide the life of a nun is unbearable, and want to leave, you will always be welcome at home."

Both women are in tears as they embrace one another. Sange comes over and nods his head in approval. Miho takes out the prayer beads and hands them to her parents. She asks them to give one to her brother Shiso. In a separate furoshiki, she has five more beads for Masahiro, Masako, and their three children. She tells them this is the last gift she will be able to give them. From now on, she will be living a life of poverty.

Miho begins to cry as she watches her brother Masahiro and his family approach. They smile and embrace her.

Masako says, "Miho, you are an inspiration to me. This life you have chosen is going to be challenging but fulfilling. I admire you very much. It is an honour to be your sister-in-law. You have my full support."

Masahiro nods his head and says, "Miho, you have always been a wonderful sister. As long as you are happy, I am happy. If you ever need anything, do not hesitate to come to me."

The children gather around as Miho gives them the prayer beads as her final gift. She shows them how to hold and pray. The children thank Miho for the present and hold their beads in awe. Masahiro and Masako bow in their final tribute to their sister, who is now a nun.

The sun is beaming down, and Miho closes her eyes and lifts her head upwards. She is crying, but it is not for the sadness she felt a week ago. Now she is crying in happiness. Her family has accepted her new life, and she is grateful. She still worries about Shiso, but she will have to convince him another day. She hopes he will welcome her as a Buddhist nun and not just as his worldly sister.

The orphanage will take two months to erect, and Miho tells her family she will be going back and forth from the temple. She will be coming to help at the orphanage once a week. She hopes she will be able to see them at that time. Miho says she cannot visit them at home and can only visit for a few minutes at the orphanage. She says she cannot meet them whenever they wish because it will not be fair to the other nuns. Miho says she may only be able to wave and not converse.

A few months later, the orphanage is up and running. Miho is at the facility. She is surrounded by orphaned children and telling them a story. They are sitting on the benches in the courtyard. It begins to rain, and she herds the children back into the orphanage. As she scurries towards the door, she feels a hand pulling her back. She looks into the face of her brother Shiso. He does not look happy!

"Shiso, what are you doing here? I am sorry, but I cannot take the time to visit. I will need to get permission before I can talk to you. You can come inside out of the rain and wait in the lobby."

"Miho, I am not going to wait. I just want you to know I do not accept your lifestyle. I have come to return the prayer beads you have given me. I don't want it, and I didn't want to throw it away. I will never understand your way of thinking, and I don't want to be your brother anymore. Have a good life."

Shiso turns and runs down the roadway. Miho stands frozen with tears running down her face. She feels like her heart is breaking, and the agony is piercing. She sits down onto the floor, and her sobs rack her body, and she feels a hand on her shoulder, and she thinks Shiso has returned. She looks up, smiling, but it is the head nun. She looks at Miho with sympathy and understanding. She lifts Miho and embraces her and leads her to her prayers.

It is two years before Shiso returns to the orphanage. He is now married, and his wife cannot bear any children. He has come to the orphanage to adopt. He has waited to make certain his sister is in attendance. He asks for Miho and waits until he sees her approaching. He sees the surprised look on her face as she stops and stares.

"Shiso, what are you doing here? I thought you never wanted to see me again. Has something happened to one of the family?"

"No, everything is fine. I just came to talk to you about adoption. I am married, and my wife cannot conceive. We have decided to adopt a child. I know I said some horrible things to you, and you probably cannot forgive me. I'm truly sorry, and I need your help. Do you think you can put all the bitterness behind and introduce me to some children that need a good home? My wife Mia and I would like to adopt a boy and a girl. If possible, the younger they are, the better. Can you please help me?"

"I have no bitterness toward you. I forgave you a long time ago. Yes, I will help you adopt two children. I think it would be best if you and your wife can come here for about a week to observe. You can interact and see if you get along with any of the children. Will your wife be able to come?"

"Yes, I will talk to her. She is in accord with me about the adoption. We will return tomorrow and stay at our parent's home. I live too far away, and it will be difficult for us to travel back and forth. I know you will not be here tomorrow, but can you introduce me to the head nun and tell her my plight?"

"Come with me. We can set this adoption when you return. I will see if I can stay another day so I can be here to meet your wife."

Miho can stay one more day to process the adoption papers. A month later, her brother takes home a boy of three and a girl of one. Shiso and Mia rename the children with the names they have chosen. The boy is named Shiro and the girl Nami. Miho forgives Shiso and gives back Shiso the beads he had once returned.

CHAPTER 16

Daimyo Takayoshi is in the village for the 1660 New Year's festivities. The vendors scrub the walkways in front of their stalls, and the inns accommodate the visitors from afar.

Shina and Masako will sell one hundred rice cakes in the village square. The two women are busy rolling the rice cakes in flour and stuffing the cakes with red bean paste.

Acrobats and jugglers entertain the children, and the children receive small bags of candy. Servants carry flickering lanterns and fireflies' glow in the darkening sky. Musicians blow into bamboo flutes, and the geisha strum the koto. Dancers are on stage in beautiful costumes, and the entertainment continues for five days.

Masahiro sharpens and polishes his sword. His deceased grandfather, Mito, bequeathed his sword to Masahiro, and Masahiro fingers the revered blade lovingly. Masahiro applies powder to the blade to make it smooth and shiny.

Masahiro's mother, Mitsuko, directs the maids as they thoroughly clean the house. Mitsuko wants all the furniture waxed, and the floors mopped. Chef Mako cleans the kitchen—his domain. Masahiro's father, Sange, is at the cemetery to weed his father's grave.

Geisha Akiminiko and Maki wear their new kimonos to entertain the daimyo and his soldiers in the great hall. There is music and laughter ringing in the streets as the festivities begin.

Chef Mako is making the New Year's feast called *Osechi Ryouri*. He is marinating the salted herring roe called *kazunoko*—symbolizing prosperity. Mako is steaming the red, and white-edged fish cakes called *kamaboko*—symbolizing sunrise. Small black beans called *kuromame* simmer in soy sauce, and a person must eat at least one bean to have a long and healthy life. Mako mashes the sweet potatoes to make *kurikinton*—symbolizing treasure and victory. In a large pot, in a delicious broth, the *nimono* is cooking. It consists of various seasonal vegetables, and the contents bring stability to life. There is shredded vinegared *daikon* or white radish dish, symbolizing auspiciousness. Sometimes shredded carrots can be added to the daikon, but this year the carrot crop did not survive. A sweet egg omelet called *datemaki* symbolizes precious things.

The chef makes a special box called a *Jubako*, having seven tiers and a cover at the top. The outside of the jubako is lacquer and painted with beautiful scenes. Each tier holds prepared foods inside. On a large platter, there is a beautifully decorated sea bream called *Tai* that resembles an ocean wave as it curves. In another large ceramic dish, Mako places fresh *sashimi*. The thin slices of tuna and octopi move as though alive. In small wooden bowls, the chef puts small pieces of rice cakes called *mochi*. Mako adds a leaf of a chrysanthemum flower and a little slice of *kamaboko*. When the *ozoni* soup is ready, Mako pours a delicious soup over the rice cakes.

Daimyo Takayoshi and his troops enter Uji at eight in the evening and go to the inn to have a late supper. The meal is a grand affair, and Sange is a genial host. The daimyo's bodyguard, Mitsujiro, is sitting next to a young geisha. Daimyo Takayoshi is surprised to see Mitsujiro with a beautiful woman from the House of the Moon—a very prestigious geisha house. The daimyo gives a brisk nod and orders sake.

"Mitsujiro, I did not know where you disappeared. Why are you meeting a geisha instead of protecting me? This treatment is an insult, and I am warning you only this once. I will leave this place tomorrow afternoon, and it is up to you if you want to accompany me." says Daimyo Takayoshi in anger.

Mitsujiro hangs his head in shame.

"Please forgive me. This geisha is my sister, Hatsune, and I just found out she lives in Uji. I rushed to her side without thought. My parents are dead, and Hatsune is my only family."

"You are Mitsujiro's sister? I apologize for jumping to a false conclusion. I am Daimyo Takayoshi, and I am pleased to meet you, and if there is anything I can do for you, please ask. Your brother is always at my side to protect me. I was angered because I thought he was not fulfilling his duties, and dallying with a beautiful young maiden. Mitsujiro, I permit you to spend the rest of the night with your sister. I will see you at breakfast."

Daimyo Takayoshi glances at Hatsune and notices his heart is erratically beating. This feeling is new to him. She is a beauty with fair skin and long black hair reaching to the floor. Hatsune's almond-shaped eyes look so lost; he wants to hug her and make things right. Takayoshi quickly strides out of the room before anyone sees his attraction to Mitsujiro's sister.

Hatsune is frowning.

"What is wrong, Hatsune? I am so happy to see you, and I want you to come back home with me. I will ask Daimyo Takayoshi to give you a job in the castle. He has a daughter Hiroko, and you can teach her odori. I know you are a great classic dancer. You can also teach Hiroko deportment. Every girl should walk and sit properly, and good manners and respect are always a must. Do you think you can come tomorrow?"

"You are asking for the impossible, Mitsujiro. My geisha house will never release me without paying off my loans. I have to find a danna to give me monetary security. I'm sorry, but I cannot leave. My geisha house will send someone to bring me back, and the okiya will add more debts."

"I will ask my lord to help pay off your loan. I will promise him that I will remain by his side for the rest of my life. You need not worry. You can leave with me tomorrow when I will come to the geisha house with the money."

Mitsujiro goes to see Daimyo Takayoshi before breakfast. He begs his lord to help set his sister free. He says his sister will make an excellent companion for his daughter Hiroko. Hatsune is an accomplished classical dancer, plays the koto, sings, and can tutor his daughter in calligraphy, painting, and writing poetry.

Daimyo Takayoshi becomes angry and says, "You want a geisha as a companion for my daughter? You are out of your mind. Your sister is an entertainer and probably sleeps with many men. I will give you the money so that you can free your sister, but she will never teach my daughter. She is not welcome in the castle and must live outside its walls. You will pay me back by becoming my vassal. You must swear your allegiance to me for the rest of your natural life."

Mitsujiro agrees and borrows the money to release Hatsune. He pays off her debts and finds a small cottage for her to live. He will help her find employment, but he doesn't know where?

Lord Takayoshi frequents many pleasure quarters with his comrades. He is proud he has never once touched another woman other than his wife. He has a deep affection for Masaye and his daughter Hiroko. Now out of the blue, he desires another woman. He knows Hatsune is taboo, but Takayoshi can't get Hatsune out of his mind.

"Mitsujiro, how is your sister, and is she working? Where does she live? Do I have your permission to visit her? I want to ask Hatsune what type of employment she would like so I can help her get a job. I am sorry for implying that Hatsune is a loose woman, and I apologize for my rudeness. Please give me her address, and I will visit her tomorrow."

Lord Takayoshi wants to see Hatsune again. He dreams about her nightly, and during the day, her face appears in every woman he sees. He drinks sake before going to bed to sleep, but it doesn't help. Takayoshi is infatuated with a geisha, and he is in a quandary?

Hatsune is doing the laundry outside and does not hear the knock on her door. She is startled when she sees a man come around the corner of her cottage. She begins to scream, and the man puts his hands over her mouth to silence her. The man calmly says he is Lord Takayoshi, and Hatsune opens her eyes and sees he is telling the truth. Hatsune apologizes and gives a deep bow in embarrassment. Hatsune looks at his clothing, and it is of a peasant. She wonders why Lord Takayoshi is wearing rags.

"My Lord, why are you dressed as a peasant? It is no wonder I did not recognize you. Why are you here? Is Mitsujiro all right?"

"Your brother is fine. I didn't want to dress up and come into this part of town, and I don't want people to know I am here. I told Mitsujiro, I will help you find a job. What type of employment are you seeking?"

"There are many things I can do. I am a trained entertainer. I guess I can become a tutor for some wealthy family, and they do not have to know I was once a geisha. Do you know of a family in need of a teacher? I am well educated and can write all the Chinese characters, and I have read many books and can calculate math problems. I can recite poetry and write haiku. I think they will like my watercolor paintings of nature."

Takayoshi replies, "I told your brother that you could not live in the castle and teach my daughter. I think I was wrong. If we never tell my wife and Hiroko about your past, we should not have any problems. I think you should come three times a week to the castle to teach. We can move you into one of the castle rooms once my daughter is comfortable with your teachings. Would that be agreeable?"

Takayoshi is silently praying that Hatsune will agree to his proposal. He wants to be near her and see her every day. He wants to touch Hatsune, but he forces himself to keep away. Takayoshi doesn't want to scare Hatsune and waits for her answer.

"I guess I can try to be your daughter's tutor. I can start tomorrow if it is agreeable. I will go to the castle on Mondays, Wednesdays, and Fridays, and after a month, we can decide if you want me to be a permanent teacher. Do you have educational supplies, or do we have to buy them? I will need some art supplies, books, pens, brushes, ink, and paper. Please prepare what I need, and later we may have to buy new things. Thank you for coming today, and I look forward to meeting your wife and daughter."

Hatsune smiles and bows as Daimyo Takayoshi walks down the path into the village. He looks back and waves, and Takayoshi thinks how beautiful Hatsune is and wants to embrace her. He feels a stirring in his loins.

Mitsujiro is surprised when he hears Hatsune is going to tutor Hiroko.

"I don't understand. I thought Lord Takayoshi was completely against you teaching Midori. What changed his mind?"

"Lord Takayoshi thinks I will be a good tutor, but he wants to keep my past a secret from his wife and daughter. He wants to help me get back on my feet. I will be on trial, and I will go to the castle three days a week for one month. If everything works out, I will move into the castle and be a permanent companion and teacher. Thank you, Mitsujiro, I am excited and hope I do a good job."

Hatsune meets Hiroko and her mother Masaye, and they are gracious and welcoming. Lord Takayoshi insists Hatsune join the family for lunch before beginning Hiroko's lessons. Hatsune eats a cold noodle dish called soba. The noodles are sitting inside a basket with a broth in a round bowl. There is a dab of green horseradish to be put into the soup to make it spicy, and the cold noodles are dipped into the soup to savor. On another small plate sits some vegetable tempura. The tempura consists of deep-fried eggplant and sweet potato. Everything is delicious.

Hiroko is writing her Chinese characters and is quite good at her execution, and Hatsune is pleased. She tells Hiroko she must wash the brush and wipe it dry after each use. At three o'clock, a maid brings in tea and cake, and after a little rest, Hatsune decides to teach Hiroko how to play the koto.

The March weather is still cold, and spring will soon come. Hatsune puts on her haori and sandals to return to her cottage. Outside she finds Lord Takayoshi waiting with a rickshaw to transport her home. Hatsune thinks his thoughtfulness delightful and bows in thanks.

The following day Hatsune is free. She goes to the marketplace and is looking at some hairpins when she glances up and sees Lord Takayoshi. He smiles as he fingers a few floral kanzashi and asks Hatsune which one suits his daughter.

Hatsune looks at all the hairpins and asks what his daughter's favorite colour is? He replies she loves the color purple. Hatsune picks out three hairpins and ponders which one would suit Hiroko the best, and she decides on the dangling wisteria flower. Lord Takayoshi purchases the kanzashi and asks if she will go to the teahouse with him? Hatsune is surprised but agrees.

Sipping tea and discussing Hiroko is pleasing. Hatsune finds Daimyo Takayoshi to be an interesting conversationalist. He listens intently to her every word and seems to enjoy what she has to say. Hatsune and Lord Takayoshi agree to meet the following week at the same teahouse. Takayoshi says he wants to meet Hatsune to make sure his daughter is a diligent student.

Hiroko is intelligent and artistic. Hatsune decides to have one of Hiroko's paintings put into a frame for her parents. The painting depicts the nearby mountain range with a waterfall coming down a small rock ledge. Hatsune goes to a carpenter in the village and asks him to make a frame.

Lord Takayoshi and his wife love the painting, and Masaye immediately places it on the entry wall. The wooden bamboo frame is beautiful and accentuates the artwork. Hiroko is excited to have her art displayed in such a prominent place for all to see.

Takayoshi can hardly wait for his meeting with Hatsune. He has tried to stay away during the time she has come to the castle to teach his daughter. He doesn't want anyone to suspect his interest and ruin the friendship. Takayoshi makes it a point to be gone from his house when Hatsune comes to teach. He feels guilty towards his wife, but his feelings override his guilt.

It is finally Wednesday, and Takayoshi rushes to the teahouse. He is early and orders tea and some sweets. He stares out into the garden and watches a bee buzz about. The bee goes from one chrysanthemum plant to another, and the beautiful mums of yellows, oranges, and browns are in full bloom. Takayoshi asks the maid if it would be possible to cut one bloom to give to his guest. The maid receives the owner's permission and comes back holding a knife. The maid asks which flower Takayoshi would like cut, and he says one of the yellow blossoms.

Hatsune arrives and enters the tatami room, and Lord Takayoshi points to a cushion opposite from where he is seated. A maid is bustling about pouring fresh cups of tea. After the maid leaves, Takayoshi hands Hatsune the cut bloom. She looks surprised, and she looks up at Lord Takayoshi questioningly.

"The flower is beautiful. Why are you giving it to me? I don't understand?"

"It has no meaning. While waiting for your arrival, I thought you might like a bloom, and did not mean to offend you."

"No, not at all. *Domo arigato gozaimashita*—thank you very much. Today is the first time I have received such a meaningful gift. The flower is truly a beautiful work of nature, and I appreciate your gesture. I hope this means I am an adequate tutor, and you will hire me permanently?"

"Of course, but it is still early, and the trial time is not yet complete. We will meet weekly to compare notes. I hope my daughter is worthy of your teachings. If there is any problem, no matter how small, I would like you to report to me as soon as possible. Please call me Takayoshi and let us not be so formal."

"That is an impossible request. You are the Daimyo of the Ouchi Clan. I cannot ever call you Takayoshi when your status is greater than mine."

"Let us make a pact, and you can call me Takayoshi, only when we meet at this teahouse. You are my employee, as well as a friend. When we meet outside, you can refer to me as Lord Takayoshi. Is that agreeable to you?"

Takayoshi wants Hatsune to call him by his name with no honorifics. He wants to hear his name from her lips, and he wants to hold her hand and draw her near. Takayoshi moves his body to alleviate the stirring in his loins, and he is becoming more frustrated and needs to claim her as his own. Lord Takayoshi abruptly stands and says he has an important meeting that he has to attend and will see her the following week. Hatsune worries she has offended Lord Takayoshi by refusing to call him by his name.

It is raining heavily as Lord Takayoshi waits for Hatsune to come, and the sound of the rain is steady and loud. The hour to meet comes—but Hatsune does not appear. Takayoshi paces the room and becomes alarmed. He worries that she has been in an accident. Was she ill? Takayoshi goes to the front entry and asks if a message has arrived for him. There is no message, and he returns to the guest room and waits. After two hours, he leaves to go to Hatsune's cottage.

Takayoshi knocks on the door, and when Hatsune doesn't answer, he begins to pound on the door. He decides to enter without permission, and senses something is wrong, and he needs to get inside. He breaks the lock and pushes the door open. Takayoshi searches the small cottage and finds Hatsune unconscious on the bedroom floor, and he picks her up and lays her onto her futon. He goes to the kitchen to get some water and a towel. Takayoshi gently wipes the perspiration from her face and neck. Takayoshi decides to undress Hatsune and takes off her kimono and her damp undergarments. Hatsune begins to shiver in the cold air. Takayoshi wipes down Hatsune's body and lies down beside her to keep her warm. His concern aside—he sexually awakens, and Takayhoshi begins to stroke Hatsune's body.

Takayoshi looks at Hatsune's nude body and finds her pale breasts are small but pleasing. He begins to pinch her nipples as she lets out a low moan. His hands travel down to the vee between her legs, and he spreads her thighs apart. Takayoshi knows he should stop, but he is at a place of no return. He feels guilty seducing Hatsune when she is ill. Lord Takayoshi meets Hatsune's eyes staring into his face, and he quickly rolls away, embarrassed, and covers Hatsune with her quilt.

"What are you doing here, my Lord?" Hatsune questions.

Takayoshi explains that Hatsune was unconscious, and he undressed her because her clothes were wet from her fevered perspiration. Takayoshi says he will get a doctor and rushes out of the cottage.

An hour later, Takayoshi returns. The doctor gets his acupuncture needles and begins to insert them into her body. Hatsune cries out whenever the needle hits a spot that causes her pain. The doctor thinks Takayoshi is Hatsune's husband and asks him to sponge her body. Takayoshi prays, the doctor does not recognize him and continues to play the role of

Hatsune's husband. Takayoshi pays the doctor and sends him on his way, and Hatsune falls asleep exhausted. Takayoshi brings a pitcher of water and leaves it by Hatsune's bed. Takayoshi's sexual urges have vanished, and he wants to depart. He hopes Hatsune will not remember his sexual overtures, and if she does, he will tell her she must have been dreaming. Takayoshi leaves a short letter saying he will send her brother Mitsujiro to watch over her for the next few days.

It takes a week before Hatsune returns to the castle to give Hiroko her lessons. She has lost weight and is very pale. Lord Takayoshi goes on a business trip, hoping Hatsune does not remember his sexual advances during her illness.

Takayoshi is traveling inspecting his domain. He stays away from home and Hatsune for four months. It is now autumn, and the trees are turning colours, and the golden and red leaves are on the ground.

Takayoshi returns home, and Masaye is overjoyed and runs outside to greet her husband. Hatsune and

Hiroko are deep in calligraphy lessons when they hear the horses and rush to the courtyard. Takayoshi steps from his mount and gathers Hiroko and Masaye into his arms. He glances at Hatsune and smiles. Takayoshi wants to hug Hatsune, but not in front of his wife and daughter.

Hatsune stays for supper. Takayoshi says he wants to hear all about Hiroko's progress in the four months he traveled. Takayoshi looks around the table, and the three women he loves the most are sitting next to him. Takayoshi wonders how long his longing for a forbidden fruit can go on.

Masaye watches the interaction between Takayoshi and Hatsune. She notices her husband's indirect glances at the beautiful woman, and Masaye notes that Hatsune seems oblivious to his feelings. She must put a stop to this before her family breaks apart. Masaye loves her husband and daughter and does not need anyone interfering in their married life. Masaye wonders if she has lost her husband's love and decides to warm his bed tonight and welcome him home.

Hiroko is happily telling her father of her progress in her studies. She says Hatsune is an excellent teacher, and she enjoys all the lessons she disliked before. Hatsune is embarrassed when Takayoshi glances her way, and Hatsune notices that Masaye is silent, and not taking part in any conversation. Hatsune decides she has taken up enough of the family's private time and excuses herself to return to her room. Hatsune moved into the castle while Lord Takayoshi was away.

Masaye takes a bath and puts the scent of gardenias on her body. She lies naked under her quilt, waiting for her husband to come to bed. It is well past one in the morning when Takayoshi appears, and he undresses and puts on a yukata, a cotton kimono, and opens the quilt to lie down. He gasps as he sees his wife completely naked, and Masaye has never done such a thing in their long-wedded life. Looking startled, he tries to leave, but Masaye pulls him down.

"What is this? What are you doing? Why are you naked?"

Masaye does not say a word. She settles back against the pillow and decides to show her husband by action. Masaye pulls Takayoshi to her side as she opens his kimono. She reaches for his manhood, and Masaye begins to move her hands up and down the velvety head. Takayoshi is no longer protesting and groans as he gathers Masaye into his arms. Takayoshi begins to knead Masaye's breasts as she continues stroking.

Takayoshi does not know why Masaye is acting out because she has always let him take the lead in their lovemaking. He wonders what has changed. He decides he will enjoy the sexual advances of his wife, and Takayoshi shudders as his seed spills out. Takayoshi knows he needs to satisfy Masaye, and begins to tend to her needs. He again begins to feel his manhood growing, and he feels like he is sixteen once more. They make love numerous times, and he looks at his wife with a deep feeling of awe. As the night deepens, they blissfully fall into each other's arms in slumber.

In the early dawn, Takayoshi awakens with his wife rubbing up against his body. She is insatiable, and he stares at her in wonder. Suddenly he thinks about Hatsune and can't believe he has not had one thought about her during this time with his wife. He is happy that whatever he felt about Hatsune was for only a fleeting moment. His guilt disappears, and he continues in their lovemaking. Masaye feels assured she has won back all of her husband's affection. She hopes all his fantasies are gone, and she will remain his one true love.

CHAPTER 17

The hail is coming down in sheets onto the rooftops of the castle. The wind is howling, and the November temperature is dropping. It is the winter of 1661. Daimyo Takayoshi is going to Uji for a meeting with his clansmen. The soldiers are in ready as Takayoshi mounts his horse, and his is bodyguard, Mitsujiro, hands him his sword. Takayoshi rides out with twenty of his soldiers.

Sange is polishing his sword, and Mitsuko is directing the maids in cleaning the house. Masahiro and Masako are tending to their children. The heavy snow is coming down, and they are snowbound.

The children are restless, so Masahiro decides to take them outside to play in the snow. Masako is bundling them up to keep them warm. She gives them a sip of hot tea to warm their little bodies.

Masako warns Masahiro to come inside within thirty minutes.

Snowballs are thrown as the children laugh in glee. Masahiro begins to build a snowman and makes a samurai warrior with a topknot on its head. Masahiro reaches into his pocket and withdraws two pieces of wood for the eyes. He sticks a piece of burdock root or gobo to use as a nose. The children giggle as they notice the snowman is lacking a mouth. Masahiro shrugs his shoulders and asks if any of the children have anything to use? His daughter Midori hands him a piece of red silk from her doll's dress. The boys laugh and say that a snowman is a man and not a woman.

The guard at the front gate interrupts Sange and hands Sange a message. It is a note summoning him to a meeting at the town hall. Daimyo Takayoshi will arrive later this afternoon and orders Sange to attend. They need to plot and be ready in the event of an attack. The villagers are restless, and a spy has told the daimyo to prepare for a revolt. The samurai sheds are full of rice, but the villagers are starving to death.

A dog on the way to the castle attacks Sange. The mongrel bites him on the leg and hand as he tries to shake the dog off. Sange is unable to wield a sword or a bow. It will be a few months before he can fight again.

Sange tells the daimyo he is going to release ten sacks of rice to the villagers. He and Masahiro will give one small basketful to each family. He wants the soldiers to keep order, so there will be no rioting. Daimyo Takayoshi thanks Sange for his generous and brilliant idea. Sange's generosity will put off the revolt today, but someday another riot will be in the making.

Masahiro and Sange are standing on the outskirts of Uji. The villagers are standing in a long line, waiting for their rice. A woman begins to cry out. She is asking for a larger portion.

"I have ten people in my family, and one portion will not be enough. I take care of my parents, my in-laws, my husband, and four children. I don't need to eat, but I have to feed the other members of my family. Please have mercy and help me?"

Masahiro asks the other villagers if she is telling the truth, and everyone nods yes. They say she has been taking care of her family for the last five years. Her husband has a disability and cannot work. The in-laws and her parents are too elderly and are not much help. The children beg on the streets for scraps of food. The woman takes in laundry and sews clothes. The villagers wonder when she sleeps. Everyone sees her working from dawn to dusk.

Masahiro hands the woman a half-sack of rice, and Masahiro offers to carry it to her house. She bows and thanks him and leads him to a shack she calls home. The house looks like it is ready to fall, and the roof has holes, and there are pails to catch the rain when there is a storm. The woman's husband is in bed, unable to walk, and the stench of his body waste is stifling. The two elderly couples are sitting around a small table, huddled for warmth. The children are in rags, and their hair is stringy and full of lice. Masahiro is appalled with the living conditions and decides he must help them.

The following day, Masahiro and Masako make their way to the Kimura house with one of their servants pulling a small cart. Inside the wagon are vegetables, chicken, and clothing. They are also bringing firewood and herbal tonics. The Kimura family is so grateful when Masahiro and Masako leave; they keep their heads lowered in thanks until they are out of sight.

Masahiro and Masako look at their children as they sleep. Their children are lucky to have clothes and a warm bed. Their stomach is full of delicious food and drink, and they want for nothing. Masako says tomorrow she is bringing some toys for the Kimura children. Masahiro says he is taking a carpenter to repair their roof.

CHAPTER 18

Sange gets a message that Daimyo Takayoshi's castle is under attack. He and Masahiro don their armor and join other clansmen on their way to the castle. The warriors said goodbye to their families and assure them they will return. The women and children have tears flowing from their eyes as they wave farewell. Many of the samurai will not survive.

When Sange and Masahiro reach the castle, it is on fire, and the enemy is shooting fire-arrows from the rooftops. The Ouchi clansmen total one hundred and twenty, and Sange estimates the enemy to be around one hundred. Sange prays the Ouchi warriors can overrun their enemies and win the siege. The lower-ranking-samurai are attacking the upper-ranking-samurai in the castle.

The lower-samurai surrounds the castle and cuts off all essential supplies to the people inside. Masahiro is a great strategist, and he splits the clansmen into four parts and asks each group to pick a leader. Masahiro sends each group into the forest to wait for the order to attack. The enemies do not notice the arrival of the Ouchi clansmen.

Masahiro sends a band of ten men into the castle grounds through a secret passage. Inside, Lord Takayoshi's soldiers are waiting for the assault. The soldiers suddenly see shadows of the Ouchi clansmen, and Masahiro's men shout out a warning.

"Stop! We are on your side. We are from the Ouchi Clan. Put down your weapons. Our leader has sent us to assess the strength of the castle."

More than half the soldiers inside the castle are injured or dead. A doctor is tending to their injuries with little hope of recovery.

The soldiers look at the samurai in surprise. They see ten men with ready swords standing against the inner castle walls. Door swings open, and Daimyo

Takayoshi steps out, and the samurai bow to their superior in respect.

"Did Masahiro send you? Thank you for coming to our aid."

It is midnight, and everything is quiet. The enemy camps out in front of the castle gate, and they have a bonfire to keep warm. The enemy is pacing up and down the outside walls, and Masahiro stealthy takes a peek at their equipment and arsenal. Masahiro knows the enemy has depleted many of their arrows, and he wants to know how many they have left. Masahiro is satisfied with what information he gathers and returns to the woods.

Masaye and Hiroko are wearing their maid's clothing. They hope the enemy will think they are servants and let them go. Hatsune has changed into Masaye's silk kimono to pose as Lord Takayoshi's wife. Daimyo Takayoshi sends his wife and daughter to safety. He is using the same secret tunnel that the samurai entered.

The Ouchi clansmen are waiting patiently in the forest. They are surprised when they see two women approaching.

"Stop, why are you coming from the castle? Who are you?"

"We are maids from the castle and trying to escape. Please let us through."

Sange approaches and looks into Masaye's eyes. He recognizes her immediately.

"Aren't you Daimyo Takayoshi's wife?"

"No, you are mistaken. You probably remember me when I previously served you when you came to visit. My name is Hinako, and I am a maid."

Sange replies, "Masaye-sama, you need not fear us. We are here to rescue the Daimyo and the people inside the castle. I am Lord Sange from Uji. Don't you remember me?"

Masaye sinks to her knees. "Yes, I recognize you, and thank you for coming to rescue us. I am so sorry to have told you a lie. I was so frightened and thought you were the enemy. Please forgive me."

Sange says, "There is nothing to forgive, and it must be terrifying for you and your daughter. I hope we have come in time. My son Masahiro is leading the rescue mission, and we are waiting until dawn before we strike. Please let me take both of you further into the forest where you will be safe."

For the past few years, the upper-ranking-samurai dominate the lower-ranking-samurai. The upper and lower-samurai have to wear different clothes so others can tell them apart. The lower-samurai are not allowed to wear wooden clogs. Only the upper–samurai can wear silk kimono. The lower-samurai want these discrepancies eliminated, and they are willing to fight for their rights.

Hours later, when the moon begins to set, Masahiro leads the attack. The sun is rising, and the sun's rays shine into the enemy's eyes. They are blinded. Masahiro slowly draws his razor-sharp blade from his scabbard. He knows the upper-samurai will never agree to unite with the lower-samurai. Twenty seconds after the fighting begins, Masahiro brings the blade down onto the head of one of his enemies.

The Ouchi Clan slashes at the lower-samurai as the lower-samurai begin to tremble in fright. Blood is flowing everywhere, and the lower-samurai can no longer counter the blades rushing toward them.

An assailant leaps out of the darkness and charges at Masahiro. At this moment, Masahiro knows he must cut down this man or die. They stare coldly at one another as they circle. The assailant holds his sword in both hands—blocking Masahiro's thrust. Masahiro brings the blade crashing down toward the head of the assailant, and sparks fly as the two blades clash. The assailant's sword becomes severed at the hilt, and the enemy knows he can die, and he throws his broken sword at Masahiro and charges him with brute force. Masahiro is on the ground, and his enemy is on top. Just as Masahiro pierces the assailant's heart, he apologizes and asks for forgiveness.

"*Mokoto ni moshiwake gozaimasu,* I am very sorry. *Watashi o yurushitei kudasai,* Please forgive me."

"Stop!" Sange yells. "Or you will die! I will cut you! Are you prepared to die here alone? You will not have any friends or family here, and you are risking not having a proper burial."

Sange deflects a blade as he fights furiously, and he delivers the deathblow to his enemy. The ground is a flowing river of blood. Blood spurts from the dying man's face as Sange completely severs his head.

One of the lower-ranking-samurai drops to his knee before Sange and begins to plea for his life. Sange watches him with eagle eyes. Suddenly the man reaches for his small knife and tries to attack Sange. It is at this moment, Sange knows he must cut down this man or else die himself. As Sange and the lower-samurai stare coldly at one another, Sange strikes. The cold steel of his sword finds its mark, and with one stroke, Sange severs the man's head. Bodies are falling everywhere as the swords cut through to the bones of the enemy. It is a bloodbath.

"Sange whispers, "It is a complete waste of human life."

The enemy surrenders in mere minutes and the leaders lay down their swords. The leaders will die without trial, and the followers will go into exile.

The attempt at defeating the Ouchi Clan fails. There is nothing but silence as Masahiro sheaths his sword.

Daimyo Takayoshi invites Masahiro to the castle. Masahiro places his sword next to a brazier holding a steaming kettle and sits opposite Daimyo Takayoshi.

Daimyo Takayoshi rewards Masahiro with the Rising Sun Badge of Honour. He holds a victory party, roasting a large boar, and kegs of sake are broken open. Many people died, but the castle survived, and Lord Takayoshi, his wife, and daughter are alive. He thanks Sange for keeping his family safe.

CHAPTER 19

A black lacquered palanquin comes through the castle gates, and on the door, the Ouchi crest is gold. The daimyo and his wife are going to the seaside for the week, and twenty soldiers will be accompanying them. Mitsujiro will be at the daimyo's side, but Hatsune will remain in the castle. Hiroko will also stay behind to study. It is a lovely brisk day in December of 1661.

Masaye is thrilled she is on a trip with Takayoshi for an entire week. The vacation will be the first time her husband takes her on a trip other than their honeymoon. Masaye loves her husband, and she prays Takayoshi will never leave her side.

The coastline is beautiful. Small sailing ships are riding the waves, and fishermen are catching their bounties with large nets. Masaye and Takayoshi stroll in the sand, and Mitsujiro lags to protect.

The moon shines down in the clear night as Masaye and Takayoshi lie in bed. They have taken a bath together, and Takayoshi is ready to make love. He takes off his robe and leans over his wife. Masaye pretends to be asleep, and Takayoshi sighs and lies back down in disappointment. Suddenly, Takayoshi feels a hand stroking his manhood. He looks over at his wife, and Masaye has a mischievous look on her face.

Takayoshi grins and begins to stroke Masaye's breasts and suckles her nipples as she gasps. He moves down her body and licks her navel and thighs, and Masaye starts to moan. Takayoshi has only had sex with his wife in the missionary style, and he wants to try something new, but he doesn't want to offend Masaye.

Masaye decides to take the initiative. She reads sex books in the castle library, but the books are taboo, and Masaye hides them between novels. The books are full of explicit drawings and instructions. At first, she was appalled at the sketches, but later became intrigued. She was frustrated and resorted to masturbation while her husband was away. Now she decides to try a new sexual position to seduce her husband.

Takayoshi places his tongue into Masaye's mouth, and he is becoming more and more aroused. He parts Masaye's legs and begins to stroke her folds, and he feels a rush of dampness. He begins to rise above her, but Masaye has other ideas. Suddenly Takayoshi is on his back, and his wife is straddling him. Masaye uses her hand to help his manhood enter, and she pushes downwards. Masaye begins to move, as Takayoshi looks dumbfounded. Takayoshi finally returns the movement as he watches his wife's face climaxing. Takayoshi feels a rush he has never felt before, as he spills his seeds. He is overwhelmed and quickly falls asleep.

Masaye wakes to the songs of birds outside her bedroom window. She stretches as she envisions her husband's lovemaking. Her face has a slight blush, and she knows she has regained her husband's love.

The following day, Masaye and Takayoshi never leave the bedchamber. Takayoshi finds his little wife has many tricks up her sleeves. They forget to eat breakfast and lunch. By late evening they are famished, and they ask the cook to make dinner. After a cup of sake, they return to their bedchamber.

Takayoshi is so satisfied he is exhausted. He can't believe Masaye's energy and passion. He wonders where she has learned all the sexual positions. Has she had sex with other men while he was gone? He suddenly is angered and storms into the bathhouse where Masaye is relaxing and bathing.

"Masaye, where did you learn all your lovemaking techniques? Are you sleeping with other men? Answer me!"

Masaye begins to laugh and replies, "Yes, I sleep with many men while you travel. Do you think they make good tutors? Do you think I was a good student? Answer me."

Masaye looks into her husband's face and realizes he is angry. She decides to stop her joking and tell him the truth.

"Takayoshi, how can you think I sleep with other men? I only love and desire you. I am reading books in the castle library. I don't know if you know, but there are many drawings and instructions there. I wanted to make you happy and still desire me after all these years of marriage. Please forgive me if you thought I was unfaithful."

Takayoshi is speechless. He can't believe Masaye is reading the 'Kama Sutra.' He appreciates that she has gone to such extremes to satisfy him. Takayoshi bends down and kisses Masaye on the mouth.

The week flies by, and the couple is in total bliss. It is time to return to the castle, and they step into the palanquin hand in hand. They are more in love than the first day of their marriage.

CHAPTER 20

Lord Takayoshi and Hatsune enter his office, and he asks about his daughter. Hatsune says Hiroko is an exceptional student and wise beyond her years. Takayoshi asks if Hatsune would like to meet a suitor and marry one day. She says no, and plans to become a nun when she turns forty.

"A nun? Why would a beautiful woman want to become a nun? You will be throwing your life away. What a waste! I can introduce you to dozens of men who would make you a perfect husband. Let's forget about your idea and let me show you how wonderful it would be to meet someone you can love."

"Thank you, Lord Takayoshi, and I am grateful you want to help me. I am already studying to become a nun. I have gone to the monastery and pledged my vow. When I turn forty years of age, I will leave all my worldly goods, and disappear from this castle. I hope you can understand my dedication to the Buddha? I will remain a virgin to the end of my life. I thank you for leaving me a virgin, many years ago. I have not forgotten and remember the time well."

Takayoshi is stunned. He hoped Hatsune did not remember the time she was ill. He is happy he had come to his senses and not violated her body. He nods his head and wishes her well.

Hiroko is becoming quite an artist, and people are clamoring for her artwork. She is receiving letters from near and far to purchase her pictures. Hatsune has become her manager, and Hatsune frames the drawings and sets the prices for the artwork. Hatsune decides to have a private showing and asks Lord Takayoshi to rent a space for the exhibit. Hatsune will hire a caterer to provide food and drinks.

It is the first week in March of 1662, and the exhibit is in full swing. The morning air is crisp, and the sun illuminates the sky of deepest blue. The upper-class society is eating and drinking in the large town hall. Hiroko's paintings grace the walls, and each has a short description and a price tag. Hiroko wears a beautiful silk purple kimono and gold gilded obi. Lord Takayoshi has guards stationed at all the entrances and exits to ensure privacy and no thievery. Hatsune is wearing a sky blue silk kimono and navy striped obi. She is fluttering around, making sure the buyers are well informed about the paintings. Masaye is sick at home with the flu and is unable to attend.

At the stroke of midnight, suddenly, the weather turns foul. Raindrops begin to fall, and the lightning starts to streak against the moonless sky. The reception is over, and the guests prepare to leave, and Mitsujiro arrives to carry the women to their palanquins and rickshaws. Hatsune doesn't want the patron's kimono ruined in the rain puddles. The men walk to their conveyances, and everyone is full of food and drink as they merrily depart with their purchases.

The money for the paintings goes into two leather saddlebags, and a large embroidered cloth covers the bags. Lord Takayoshi hands it to two soldiers to guard. Hiroko and Hatsune step into their palanquin and take three unsold paintings home. They tuck the artwork behind their seat and pull their haori around their shoulders to keep warm. Lord Takayoshi is mounted on his horse and leads the way. He dismisses his soldiers so as not to bring attention to his group. He tells the soldiers with the saddlebags to stay behind the palanquin, acting as guards.

Lord Takayoshi sees the castle in the distance and realizes they are almost home. All of a sudden, a man appears dressed in all black with a mask covering his face. He brandishes a small knife and demands the money for the paintings. Hatsune lets out a scream and pulls down the man's mask.

The man becomes disconcerted and leaps from the palanquin and disappears from view. Hatsune is hyperventilating as she recalls the handsome thief's face. She knows she will never forget the beautiful brown almond-shaped eyes as he threatened. Lord Takayoshi leaps from his horse and opens the palanquin door. Hatsune screams again, thinking the thief has returned. Hiroko explains that a man tried to rob them, and Takayoshi is surprised that he had not seen the man. He concludes the man must have been a ninja to be so invisible. He questions the two soldiers behind the conveyance, and they, too, did not see anyone.

Hiroko finds her mother burning with fever. Steam is coming out of an iron kettle sitting on a firepot called a hibachi. The room is warm, but her mother says she is cold and is shaking. Hiroko makes a cup of tea and begins to spoon it into her mother's mouth.

The shoji screen opens, and a masked man dressed in black enters. Hiroko gasps as she recognizes him as the thief inside the palanquin. Hiroko is ready to scream when the thief puts his hand to his lips and warns her not to make any sound. There is a shuffling at the door, and Hatsune calls out to Hiroko.

"How is your mother? Is she feeling better? Do you want me to come in and help you?"

The man whispers, "Tell her to come in."

Hiroko calls out, "Please enter."

The intruder goes to the side of the door as Hatsune enters. He grabs her and covers her mouth with his hand. She struggles, but he is too strong. He tells her to keep silent and sit down. Hatsune obeys and worries about the safety of Hiroko and Masaye.

"Where is the money? I promise not to hurt you if you hand over the coins. If you do not tell me, I will kidnap one of you for ransom."

He throws back his head and roars with laughter.

"Now, which one of you ladies is the most important to the daimyo? I think it must be you," he points to Hiroko.

Hatsune says, "No, she is not. I am Takayoshi's wife and lover. This girl is not our daughter. Her mother is this woman lying here sick. They are devoted servants that have been with me many years.

My maid might be dying and in need of a doctor. I came to check on them, and you grabbed me. Who are you, and what do you want?"

Luckily, Hiroko is no longer in her elaborate kimono and wears a nondescript yukata. Hatsune still has on her elegant silk kimono, and the intruder decides Hatsune must be the wife. The intruder tells Hiroko to tell her master a messenger will come with the ransom amount.

Hiroko runs from the room to find her father. He is looking over his estate papers. He looks up as she runs into the room.

"Is your mother all right? You look a fright. Do you want me to get a doctor?"

"Oka-san is still ill, and perhaps a doctor can help. That is not the reason I'm here. The same masked man that was in our palanquin took Hatsune away. Hatsune protected mother and I and said she was your wife, and the kidnapper think we are only the servants. Please help her. You are supposed to wait for a message where to send the ransom money."

Takayoshi shouts for Mitsujiro, and he arrives out of breath.

"Yes, my lord. What can I do for you?"

"Mitsujiro, I have bad news. The kidnapper thinks Hatsune is my wife and is holding her for ransom. You must send some of the soldiers in search of her as soon as possible. We don't have a minute to lose. The intruder left only fifteen minutes ago, so they must still be near. Hurry!"

A peasant boy delivers a ransom note. He is demanding thirty gold coins called Ryo. Takayoshi questions the boy and asks if he knows where the man lives? The boy says a man gave him a coin to deliver the message and he has never seen him before. Takayoshi tells the boy if he sees the man again to come and report to him. He gives him a coin and tells him he will receive another if he can tell him where to find the kidnapper.

They pay rice taxes. During this samurai period, either rice or Chinese coinage is the same as money. Sometimes other crops are used to pay their debts.

Takayoshi has a few available coins, but he will have to ask the shogun for more money. The shogun is a general and effectively the ruler of Japan. The daimyo is powerful nobles who have control over their regions and answers to the shogun. The samurai are warriors who are faithful to the daimyo and maintain control over their daimyo region for them. The warriors also collect taxes and run the estates.

Hatsune steps into a run-down palanquin and trips because she is blindfolded. The kidnapper is slender and tall. His long black wavy hair is tied back to the middle of his head with a small black ribbon. His clothes are all black. Hatsune suspects he is a ninja warrior.

It is dawn before they reach a house in the countryside. There is a guard at the gate holding a spear. He, too, is dressed in all black. He calls out a greeting.

"Goro, you're back? Who is the woman you have with you? Is she your new girlfriend? Don't let

Megumi see her. It's a good thing she isn't here right now. She went to the mountain to pick mushrooms."

"Kenji, mind your own business. My prisoner is Daimyo Takayoshi's wife. I'm holding her for ransom. I have asked for money and tomorrow I will send them the location where they need to bring the money. Put her in the storage shed and keep her under guard."

The following morning Hatsune watches the ninjas through the cracks of the shed. There are over fifty men all dressed in black. They are in the field practicing spear techniques, and the men wrestle without any weapons. Ninja men only use agility and martial discipline. To Hatsune's surprise, she notices there are twenty women on horseback. Hatsune watches them as they disappear under the sides of the horses. The ninja women are agile and do jumps over logs and fences. They, too, are dressed in black clothing, and their shoulder-length hair ties back at the base of the neck with a black ribbon. The women are wiry and tiny.

The men begin to practice throwing a small weapon called a shuriken in the shape of a star. Hatsune is familiar with the weapon because her brother once had one piercing his arm. The men are throwing the shuriken against a tree in the meadow and are throwing tasseled spikes. The women are lighting smoke bombs and hurling them towards a sandy piece of ground. Hatsune guesses the sandy land avoids any fire to spread. Hatsune becomes fascinated with the disciplined men and women and wishes she could be one of them.

Goro comes into the meadow unmasked, and Hatsune admires his beautiful almond-shaped eyes. Goro's shoulder-length hair is wildly hanging, and Hatsune notices his muscular chest and arms. Goro begins to spar with one of the woman ninjas and treats the woman like a man.

The morning is over, and Hatsune is hungry. No one has brought her breakfast. Goro comes over to the shed to check on her. She complains that they are savages and have not fed her. He looks surprised, and he walks into a nearby tent and comes out with a bowl of soup and rice. He unlocks the shed and hands her the food.

Hatsune begins to question Goro about ninja life. She is curious and wants to be told all about the organization. She knows absolutely nothing about them—only they are a secret establishment.

Goro laughs and begins to explain, "We are covert agents or mercenaries and involved in espionage, deception, and surprise attacks. The samurai do not like the way we wage our irregular warfare and deem us to be dishonourable and beneath them. The ninja is in constant training, and we are stealth soldiers hired mostly by the daimyo. The ninja also assassinates people as part of our job. Although the samurai class hates us, the ninja is necessary for warfare, and the samurai hire us to work. We carry out operations that are forbidden by the bushido, and the ninja are not murderers, as many people believe. The ninja is trying to bring peace and harmony and doing a service no one else wants to perform.

The ninja first emerged as mercenaries in the fifteenth century and was recruited as spies, raiders, arsonists, and terrorists. The word ninja derives from the Japanese characters "nin" and "ja." Originally "nin" meant "persevere," but over time, it changed to stand for "conceal" and "move stealthily". In Japanese, "ja" is the combining form of sha, meaning "person." The ninja originated on the mountain of Japan over two hundred years ago.

The first ninja leaders were called "shinobi." Many of the ninja leaders were disgraced samurai warriors that were too cowardly to commit suicide and had fled. Most of the ninja were not from the nobility and instead were villagers and farmers. Women also served as ninja combatants. Female ninja called kunoichi infiltrated enemy castles in the disguise of dancers, concubines, and servants. Earning the trust of the castle staff, the women were efficient assassins.

Throughout history, the shinobi were assassins, scouts, and spies who were hired mostly by territorial lords known as a daimyo."

Goro tells Hatsune he cannot tell her anything else about the ninja and their operations. Everything is secret, and only the people inside the compound know what the ninja does.

Hatsune responds, "I am truly impressed. I now view your group in a different light. I thought you were useless rebels always trying to disrupt order. I now believe that you and your fellow members are necessary, and I will champion you from this day forward."

Goro is happy with Hatsune's response.

Goro goes into his tent and decides to write a small leaflet about the ninja. He will share it with the members of his organization. He decides to write the booklet as though he is speaking as a teacher to a student:

When the Nightingale Sings

To hide our identities, we travel in disguises. We go into different situations where the enemy lives. We infiltrate into the middle of the enemy to discover gaps and enter enemy castles to set them on fire. We carry out assassinations in secret. We eat a vegetarian diet to keep healthy. We will not eat any foods that may cause strong body odors.

Many times we work as a team and not always alone. Teamwork techniques exist due to necessity. To scale a wall, a group of us may have to carry each other on our backs or provide a human platform to assist an individual in reaching greater heights. Ropes and grappling hooks are attached to our belts. A collapsible ladder featuring spikes at both ends anchor the ladder. Spiked or hooked climbing gear double as weapons. Other equipment includes chisels, hammers, drills, and picks.

Besides learning martial arts, our students must study survival and scouting techniques. We teach information regarding poisons and explosives. Physical training is essential. The students have to run long distances, learn how to climb, and learn to be stealthy in both walking and swimming. We must have extensive training in medicine to help our teammates if an injury occurs. We are as knowledgeable about remedies as much as a doctor.

We can pretend to be a doctor to gain vital information from a patient and their family. We can also kill our targets with poison while pretending to be applying medical attention. We can paint the poison onto our arrowheads or on the edges of our knives. Our enemies will die from the wounds caused by scratches made by our poisoned weapons. We learn to stop bleeding by using what is known as the black medicine.

We usually live deep on the mountain where various types of plants grow. We peddle medicines and travel all over Japan. Our disguises create a ruse to gather information about other territories.

Joan T. Seko

We disguise ourselves as common mountain men to travel freely between political boundaries. The loose robes of Buddhist priests help conceal weapons. Acting like a minstrel allows us to enter and spy in enemy buildings without arousing suspicion. Disguises as a monk are effective as the large basket hats conceal our heads altogether.

Many times, we go into battle wearing the same kind of clothes as the enemy. Wearing the same type of clothes confuses the enemy, they can't tell who their foe is and who is one of them. We charge backward to attack. This tactic is also a method of crowd dispersal.

The surprise is the main tactic of the ninja. We appear in the night and stab them in the low corridors or a small Japanese room. We use short small weapons and sharp strikes.

In espionage, we try to avoid open battlefields with large superior enemy forces. We like to stun the enemy and escape in case of failure. Disguises come in forms of priests, entertainers, fortunetellers, merchants, ronin, and monks. We disguise ourselves as ordinary people.

The upper society and samurai, to prevent the ninja from intruding, put a variety of countermeasures in place. Precautions are often taken against assassins by hiding weapons in the toilets or under a removable floorboard. Buildings have traps and tripwires attached to alarm bells. The designs of the Japanese castles make it challenging to navigate with their winding routes leading to an inner compound. Blind spots and holes in the walls provide constant surveillance of these labyrinthine paths. The outside walkways have "nightingale floors." They rest on medal hinges (uguisu-bari) designed to squeak when someone walks over the wooden floors. Gravel covers the ground, so the people inside are given early notice of unwanted intruders. Segregated buildings keep the fire contained.

Goro stops writing as he turns at the sound of someone coming through the gate. A woman holding a gunnysack walks into the camp. The girl speaks to one of the guards, and he points towards the shed.

"Goro, are you in the shed? I picked some pine mushrooms on the mountain. Minoru can make some delicious matsutake gohan for dinner. Where are you? Answer me!"

"Megumi, I'm in the shed feeding my prisoner. Please give the matsutake to Minoru. I look forward to a delicious dinner tonight. Thank you."

Megumi walks into the shed and looks stunned. She eyes Hatsune and haughtily tosses the sack onto the ground.

"Goro, you didn't tell me you had a woman prisoner. You shouldn't be in here with her alone. From now on, I will have Naomi feed and take care of her."

"As you wish," answers Goro. He winks at Hatsune and walks away.

Naomi brings Hatsune a dinner of pine-mushroom rice and tea. Hatsune asks Naomi for a blanket saying she was cold the night before. Naomi brings a blue and black cotton futon, and Hatsune thanks Naomi and lies down to sleep.

In the middle of the night, Hatsune hears soft footsteps. She peers out of the shed, but she can't see anything. She feels a presence around her, and she is alarmed. She looks up and sees two eyes staring down at her from the rooftop. She screams.

Naomi comes running. She has a lantern in her hand. The female ninja looks into the shed and wonders why Hatsune screamed? She questions Hatsune, and Hatsune says something or someone was looking down at her from the roof. Naomi begins to laugh and tells Hatsune that the camp is doing night training exercises. The training will teach the members to be so silent no one will suspect their presence. Hatsune is miffed and says someone should have warned her.

In the late afternoon, Megumi blindfolds Hatsune and takes her to the edge of the castle village and let loose.

Hatsune walks to the castle on the other side of town. The guard at the gate immediately lets her enter and calls out that the tutor is back. Hiroko comes running and hugs Hatsune so tightly she can barely breathe. Masaye and Takayoshi are surprised to see Hatsune because they did not pay any ransom.

"Why were you released? We did not receive a second note to tell us where to bring the gold. Perhaps they found out you are not my wife?" says Lord Takayoshi.

"It doesn't matter why they let me go. All I know is I was at some ninja compound a few hours from here. They treated me decently and blindfolded me, so I cannot tell you the location of the camp. I am happy to be alive. Do you mind if I take a hot bath and change into some clean clothes?"

Goro has taken some of the men to buy supplies. He returns after lunch and asks Naomi how the prisoner is faring?

Naomi says, "Megumi took the prisoner and hasn't returned. "

Goro storms into the shed and says, "I want to speak to Megumi as soon as she returns. She had no right to take the prisoner away. She is going to suffer disciplinary actions for what she has done today."

Three hours pass, and Megumi is finally back. She is humming a tune and smiling. Naomi beckons her to her side and tells her Goro wants to see her immediately.

"Goro, did you want to see me? I just got back from releasing the prisoner outside the castle town. I found out she is not the daimyo's wife and only a tutor for his daughter. I thought I would save you the trouble to take her back when you are so busy."

"Why did you release the woman? How dare you! You had no right to disobey my orders, and the prisoner was mine and not yours. For this disobedience, you will not be able to train with the others for the rest of the first training session. You will have to wait until next summer to continue. If this is not agreeable, you may leave the camp immediately. I will not stop you. I am disappointed you are jealous."

"Jealous? You think I was jealous of that woman?"

"Yes, you were jealous. It was very apparent when you found out I had a woman prisoner, and you objected. I had no designs on her, and you thought she would be a threat to our relationship. Well, as of this moment, we no longer have a relationship. Without trust and honesty, I cannot honour you. I thought I knew you like the back of my hand. I will not have any woman of mine going behind my back and countermanding my orders. I am the head of this camp, and if you cannot follow my orders, you can leave."

Megumi is sobbing softly. Goro is amazed because he has never seen her cry. She has always been as tough as nails and could take the pain of any man without flinching. He feels pity for her but knows he must let her go. He realizes he does not love her with unconditional love. He decides not to tell her this because he doesn't want to rub more salt into her wound.

Goro watches as Megumi exits the gate. He is sorry to see her go, but he knows he is right. He has known her since they were children, but their paths have now become divided. He says a silent farewell as he turns and goes to dinner.

Megumi is angry. She has known Goro since they were five, and she can't believe he is treating her like a stranger. She is going to pay him back. She goes to see Akira, a man that owns a gambling establishment. Akira is dishonorable, a thief, and takes part in covert operations. Akira wears a patch on his blind left eye, and Akira was twelve when Megumi witnessed the accident. Megumi was hiding behind a fence with Goro when he accidentally blinded Akira. She had sworn to Goro that she would keep the accident a secret for the rest of her life. Now since Goro has accused her of being dishonourable, she decides to prove him right. Akira has been searching all these years for the culprit that shot him. Megumi knows he will get even with Goro, and she smiles in anticipation.

"You wanted to see me? Aren't you Goro's girlfriend? I can't remember your name. What do you want? I am busy and don't have time to talk to you."

"I think you will be happy to know who blinded you with an arrow. I have kept it a secret until now. Goro is the one who made you blind. It was an accident, but he never got up the nerve to tell you. I think it is time for revenge. I will help you!"

"How do I know if you are telling the truth? Goro is the head of the secret society of the ninja. I can't afford to become his enemy. Why should I trust and believe you?"

"Goro kicked me out of the compound. He accused me of being a traitor and not trustworthy. I have been loyal to him and his cause for ten years. He is angry because I released his prisoner without getting his permission. I found out that the woman was not the person Goro thought she was but just a mere servant. He said I was jealous and vindictive. I cannot forgive his treatment, and that is why I'm here. Do you believe me now?"

"Whether I believe you or not doesn't matter. Goro may be the one who blinded me, but at least he is living his life honourably. You, on the other hand, are despicable. You promised to keep a secret, and you have betrayed your friend. I will not have any dealings with someone like you. I will always worry when you will turn on me. Go away before I do something I will regret."

"Don't you care that it was Goro that blinded you?"

"I always wanted to know, but I think of Goro as a good friend. He may have shot the arrow, but he was only five years old. Through these many years, he has repaid me tenfold. Whenever I am in trouble, he is always there to help me. Thank you for telling me so I can put the matter to rest. This truth has cleared my mind."

Megumi is disgusted. Her revenge has come to naught. She wonders what she can do now. She stomps out of the gambling hall, fuming.

Akira sends a message to Goro and says Megumi told him that Goro was the cause of his blindness. Akira warns Goro that Megumi is out for revenge. Akira says he holds no hatred against Goro, and he wants to remain friends.

Goro is incensed. He tells all the members Megumi is no longer welcome in their compound. If she should show her face, he wants her arrested and brought to him. He wonders how he could have ever loved her.

Megumi is drinking sake and getting very inebriated. She decides to make firebombs. She was the best bomb-thrower when she was in training. She makes three bombs and sets out to the ninja camp. The night is cold, and a breeze is blowing. She hopes the breeze will fan the fire and destroy the compound. There are two guards posted at the front gate. Megumi pries open a loose board and crawls into the camp. She halts as she sees Goro walking towards the supply shed—joking with one of his men. Megumi thinks to herself, who is going to have the last laugh.

Megumi decides to wait until everyone goes to bed. The guards will be the only ones awake. She hides in the shadows and waits. Goro comes out of the supply shed and stretches his arms upwards. He yawns and walks toward the camp kitchen. He comes out with a cup of tea in his hands. Megumi tries to make herself invisible. Suddenly Goro glances around and listens. With his sharp sense of hearing and smell, he detects something in the air. He lights a lantern and begins to walk around the perimeter.

Megumi holds her breath as Goro walks past her hiding place. She is dressed in all black and has smeared soot all over her face, neck, and hands. Megumi tries to be still, but her foot begins to cramp. She can feel her toes curl. The spasm is so painful she bites into the fabric of her sleeve to keep from crying out. Goro walks towards the front gate and asks the guards if they have seen anything unusual? They say everything is as it should be. Goro seems satisfied and douses the candle. He says goodnight to the guards and goes to bed.

Lightning is streaking across the gray sky, and Megumi has fallen asleep. The thunder roars, and she jerks awake and realizes the sun will soon rise. Megumi feels woozy after drinking the sake the night before. The camp is stirring, and she needs to leave before they find her. Megumi hides the three bombs in the woods until she can return to finish destroying the camp.

The rain continues for five days, and the ground is soaked and muddy. The camp continues with the training, but Megumi has to postpone her attack due to the heavy rainfall. She hopes the hidden bombs will remain in good condition until she returns.

When Megumi returns to the compound, she hears the barking of a dog. There has never been a dog in the camp before, and Megumi wonders if the dog belongs to Goro?

The presence of the dog makes it impossible for Megumi to continue her attack, and she leaves in disappointment.

A month later, the cherry trees are budding. Megumi is listless as she plots her long-awaited revenge. She decides she will attack when the sun sets. Tonight is as good as any. The April weather is warming up, and the sky is clear. She changes her clothes and sets out for the compound. She takes some chicken to feed the dog if it is still there. She is met with a loud bark as she approaches. She throws the meat, and the dog gobbles it up. She reaches into the opening of the fence and strokes the dog's ears.

Megumi finds the hidden bombs, and they are undamaged. The silence is eerie as Megumi lights one bomb and tosses it onto the thatched top of the shed, and the roof explodes as the flames grow, and Megumi throws the second bomb into the latrine. She laughs as the outhouse disintegrates, and she tosses the final bomb into the kitchen tent. She hopes no one is inside, but she is wrong, and the cook runs out with his clothes burning. Megumi races to the cook and uses her hands to beat at the flames. Megumi had no intention of hurting anyone, and she yells fire, and pandemonium follows. Megumi's hands blister, and she falls to the ground, unconscious.

Goro finds Megumi in a faint. He picks her up and rushes her to the river and dunks her into the cold water. Megumi opens her eyes, and the pain in her hands is unbearable. She stares into Goro's eyes and begins to cry.

"I'm so sorry. I didn't mean for anyone to get hurt. How is the cook? I tried to put out the fire on his clothes, but I think I was too late."

Goro looks at Megumi with pity. He can't believe she can be so vindictive. The fire spread throughout the camp, but luckily the only fatality was the cook. The compound is a total loss, and Megumi is guilty of murder.

Megumi's hanging is a solemn event, but no one mourns her passing. Everyone is angry about the senseless act she committed. She had been a revered member for ten years, and now she is dead. The ninja begins to clean up and rebuild. Goro buries Megumi in an unmarked grave up on the mountain.

CHAPTER 21

The compound smells like wet ash, and the exterior walls of the sheds and stables are blackened and charred. An entire year passes before the shinoku or ninja compound is up and running. It is now April of 1663, and Goro is teaching the recruits the art of stealth and espionage.

Goro builds a house with traps and hidden rooms and hallways. The house is full of secret entries and exits without windows and doors.

Many ninja leaders are disgraced samurai, and instead of committing the ritual suicide, they fled. Most of the ninja is not from the nobility and are villagers and farmers.

Women ninja or kunochi acted like dancers, concubines, and servants. The women are highly successful spies and infiltrate enemy castles in disguise.

The samurai warriors deem the ninja to be dishonourable and beneath them. The samurai believe the ninja is deceptive, and their covert methods are undesirable. What the samurai doesn't know is the shinobi is hired by their daimyo and shogun to assassinate and spy. The ninja is taught not to get into any fights unless necessary. The shinobi are masters of surprise attacks.

The samurai hires ninjas to do their dirty work. The ninja gives out misinformation to opponents and kills them. The samurai cannot openly join in warfare because they follow the rules of bushido. The ninja is paid handsomely by the samurai, but the samurai do not treat the ninja as equals.

Goro dresses like an old man. He is wearing a wig called a katsura. The katsura and his mustache and beard are silver in colour. His kimono is brown with a black obi. He is using a wooden cane as he limps towards the gates of the castle. The guard shouts for him to halt.

"Please tell Lord Takayoshi; Taka is here to see him. We were supposed to meet tomorrow, but I arrived a day early. I hope this will not inconvenience him. If he is unavailable, I will come back tomorrow," replies Goro.

"Teru, come here. Tell Lord Takayoshi, a man named Taka, is here to see him. Hurry and run along."

The gate opens, and Goro enters into the courtyard. Lord Takayoshi is rushing to his side.

"Taka, it is good to see you. Please come in. Mitsujiro, I don't want to be disturbed, so please seal the corridor for our privacy. Tell the maid that you will bring in sake and some light food for us to eat. Is that understood?"

"Hai," replies the bodyguard.

The two men sit on the tatami floor next to a short lacquered wooden table.

Mitsujiro returns with a bottle of sake and two cups. Goro accepts a cup of sake and places it on the table.

"I have called you to help me find someone that is trying to kill me. The person has attempted to kidnap me two times. Once when I was in the marketplace and the other time was when I exited from the Kabuki Theater. Both times I was able to escape because my bodyguard intervened."

Goro is looking at Lord Takayoshi. Lord Takayoshi seems unaware that Goro had tried to kidnap a woman he thought was Lord Takayoshi's wife. Goro was not going to harm her—he just needed the gold to fund his organization. Unfortunately, everything had gone array. Megumi had returned the tutor without permission. Now Megumi is dead.

"Can you recognize the man if you see him again. Can you describe his clothes? How tall is he? How old do you think he is? Do you remember any distinguishing marks or scars on his face or body?"

"The only thing I remember was a scar on his right hand. I saw it when he had a knife held at my neck. When Mitsujiro jumped on his back, he dropped the knife and fled."

"Mitsujiro, do you still have the knife? I would like to see it. I may be able to tell who made the knife and name the owner."

"I will go to my quarters and bring it when I bring in the food. I will be right back."

Mitsujiro hands the knife to Goro, and Goro is stunned. Goro gave the knife to Megumi as a gift on her sixteenth birthday. Was it Megumi that had attacked Lord Takayoshi? Was she in disguise as a man? Goro remembers Megumi injured her right hand during one of the exercises two years past.

"You look surprised. Do you recognize the knife?" asks Lord Takayoshi.

Goro replies, "Yes, I know the knife. The person that owned it is dead. If the assassin was the owner of the knife, she was a woman and not a man. I gave her the knife as a gift on her sixteenth birthday. She was very close to me, and I don't know why she tried to kill you? Now that she is dead, I will have to find out why? I will also have to find out if someone else will be taking her place, and you are still in danger. Unfortunately, she never confided in me about her latest covert operation. She had become a stranger to me, and she was no longer someone I could trust. She was acting strangely, and she had changed. When I leave here, I will work hard to solve this mystery. If you remember something else, let me know. I would suggest you keep your bodyguard close and try not to go out unless necessary. I will report to you as soon as I have something to tell. Thank you for the refreshments."

Goro returns to the training grounds and decides to talk to all the members. He wants to know if anyone knew about Megumi's movements. He is worried that others besides Megumi, may have infiltrated his compound. He interrogates half the men and women and becomes suspicious. A new trainee named Asako is not meeting his eyes and is acting very nervous. Goro spots the lies that are spurting from her mouth. He is a well-trained ninja, and he decides to trap her.

"How are you doing in your training? Tomio says he thinks you will never become a ninja. He says you are too slow and can't throw the spear without going in the wrong direction. Perhaps you are not meant to become one of us, and it may be better if you did not finish your lessons and find a different occupation," lies Goro.

Asako is fuming. She is already an operative with a long line of credentials. How dare this man think so poorly of her while listening to one of his incompetent trainers? As she listens to Goro, she becomes angrier.

"How dare you question my skills? I was trained and have passed all the tests at the Hiromatsu Camp in Kyushu. I was one of the best," she blurts out.

She suddenly stops and puts her hand over her mouth. She knows she has given herself away. Goro has purposely insulted her, and she has taken his bait.

Her face becomes pale as she looks at Goro's smiling face.

"Why are you here? Answer me before I send you to prison. Are you here to harm Daimyo Takayoshi? If you confess, I will make certain your jail sentence is light," responds Goro.

Asako is defeated. She sighs and slowly sinks to the ground. She decides to speak and tell Goro why she is in his compound.

"I am Megumi's older sister and went to live with my aunt when I was three. Megumi and I are orphans because Daimyo Takayoshi's father killed our parents during an uprising. We only live to seek revenge for our parent's death. Megumi made me infiltrate your camp so I could be near Lord Takayoshi's castle. Megumi will be disappointed you know our secret. Tell me where you buried her so I can visit her grave."

Goro listens and feels remorse and pity for the girl sitting in front of him.

"Listen, Asako; I have no right to condemn you. I am sorry you and Megumi lost your parents at such a tender age. I think you have forgotten it is not the daimyo's fault that your parents died. You must understand it was the villagers that revolted, and he was only trying to protect his family and himself. Besides, the present daimyo isn't to blame; he was only a boy at that time. If you promise to forget your animosity towards Daimyo Takayoshi, I will look the other way. Please join us in making life better and give up your revenge. I will take you to Megumi's unmarked grave."

Asako nods her head. "I will pledge my life to you and your ninja group. Thank you for helping me. I will be loyal to you as long as I live."

Goro goes to Daimyo Takayoshi and explains the circumstances of Megumi and Asako's revenge. He says Megumi is dead, and Asako has decided to pledge her life to Goro's group. He says Asako is no longer a threat, so he does not have to worry. Daimyo Takayoshi is relieved. He says he would like to give something to Asako for her past pain and loss. He goes to his room and comes back with a gold necklace. He hands it to Goro and asks him to deliver it to Asako. He also gives Asako a letter. In the message is a pass to enter the castle at any time she is in need.

CHAPTER 22

Goro is off at a fast trot and hurries through the woods and the dark shadows of the trees. He is tired from a night of interrupted sleep, and his nerves are on edge brought on by fatigue. He comes to the top of a hill and sees a haze and a column of smoke as it spirals upwards. Goro looks down into the valley and sees the gutted castle and fire burning out of control. As he approaches the marketplace, there are dead bodies cut to bits and blackened as they fled from the fire. Goro smells the burnt flesh and looks down at a small child holding her mother's hand. Goro searches for a sign of life and finds none. He continues towards the castle.

Reaching the main gate of the castle, Goro stops. The front wall of the castle is black, and the courtyard is on fire. Goro sees some survivors huddled in the corner. Their faces are black with soot, and their clothes riddled with holes. He picks his way through the injured and dying, and Goro sees Daimyo Takayoshi searching the courtyard looking for his family. The daimyo approaches Goro and asks for help.

"I was asleep and heard noises, and I rushed to the door, and someone pushed me aside and broke in. The man threw a spear, and I tripped on a man with his throat ripped open. I ran back inside to find my family—but they were gone."

Goro questions a soldier outside. The soldier says he saw Lord Takayoshi's wife, daughter, and tutor running away with some soldiers. He doesn't know if it was the enemy or one of Lord Takayoshi's men.

"Did you see who was attacking the castle? Did you recognize anyone?"

"Someone struck me from behind while I was standing by the back gate. When I woke, I saw ten men in black masks, killing the servants as they ran. I could see the village in flames and chaos everywhere. I don't think many people survived. I lay on the ground pretending to be dead. I have to go home now to see if my family is still alive."

Goro rides around the castle grounds and the village. The enemy is long gone. He finds villagers hiding in a horse stall where the roof and the horses are missing. He helps the villagers pile up the dead bodies and set them on fire. By nightfall, Goro is exhausted and hungry. It is going to be challenging to find food in the blackened kitchens.

Goro orders a handful of soldiers to go hunting and bring back some game. There is barely any food left in the village, and people are starving.

"Where are all the other soldiers? I thought Lord Sange had over five hundred. Where did they go?" asks Goro.

One of the soldier's replies, "The assassins killed the guards and opened the gates. They threw lit arrows into the castle and our barracks. We woke up to an inferno and tried to get to our weapons. A few escaped through the windows while others fought with their bare hands to stay alive. Too many are injured, and too many are near death. We have no medicine to administer to them."

A villager is cooking a large pot of stew in the courtyard. She hands Goro a bowl as he sits listening to the previous happenings from a soldier's lips. The soldier says there were dozens of raiders all dressed in black with masks on their faces. It was a well-planned surprise attack.

A man comes running and says he found some horses down by the river. Goro tells him to teeter them so they don't runoff. Goro decides he needs some sleep before he can continue, and he lies down in one of the roofless stalls. At sunrise, the rain comes down in sheets, and within minutes he is soaked to the skin. The rain helps smother the hot ashes, and the stench from the dead bodies still to be buried.

Goro sees two figures hidden in an abandoned shed. He moves quietly and tiptoes up behind them. He listens to their whispers, and he realizes he has stumbled onto two enemy assassins. One of the men tries to escape through the door, but Goro spins him around as he lashes out with his short knife. He wants to capture these two men alive. He needs to know who they are and why they have attacked a peaceful village and castle? He overcomes the two intruders and ties them with a rope. He drags them out to the middle of the courtyard and points to the destruction and murder they have caused. The two men try to look away, but Goro forces them to look at the dead women and children they have slaughtered.

"You are animals! These women and children could be your own family. I can understand killing the men, but I can never comprehend why you slaughtered these innocent women and children. You are worse than dogs! I can't even stand to look at you. You will be locked up and have to face your fate in the morning. Daimyo Takayoshi will decide your sentence, and you are most likely facing death. We can spare your life if you tell us everything about the attack. There is a possibility that you may be exiled and live. I suggest you think deeply about this overnight," says Goro angrily.

The following morning, the assassins are interrogated but refuse to give out any information. Daimyo Takayoshi sentences them to death and decides to starve them rather than give a quick death by beheading. The soldiers tie the prisoners to two wooden posts and take off their clothing except for their fundoshi.

The survivors spit upon the assassins as they pass by each day. To make the killers suffer more, the villagers begin to cook and eat their meals in front of them. They spill water onto the ground to taunt them.

The prisoner's throats are swollen and parched. They are in agony as the villager's tease and throw water onto the earth. They are becoming dizzy and disoriented.

"Mizu! Mizu! Water! Water!" they beg.

One villager decides to give the prisoners a sip of water each day. She says this will keep the prisoners alive longer. She wants them to suffer. The prisoners are kept alive for forty-five days. When death finally overtakes them, they are skin and bones. They are hallucinating and calling out to their loved ones. Death is a welcome end to their suffering. They are cut down and buried into an unmarked pit.

Days fly by, and slowly the village begins to rebuild. Lord Takayoshi walks in a daze, unable to find his wife and daughter. The assassins are gone leaving the village in misery. Goro sends a messenger to Lord Sange and his son Masahiro to bring help.

A week goes by, and ten wagons approach the village with Lord Sange leading the way. The wagons carry much-needed food, clothing, and building supplies.

Goro is shocked when he finds some of the weapons with his insignia lying on the ground. He can't believe the assassins were part of his group. He rushes back to his compound in disbelief.

Goro finds ten of his ninja students has disappeared. He realizes they were assassins and had used his compound as a ruse to attack the castle and village. He goes in search of Asako, who had been one of them before she had come to his side. He hopes she had not deceived him and is still in the camp.

"Has anyone seen Asako? Please tell her I would like to speak to her immediately. I need some volunteers to go to the castle and village. The assassins set a fire, and there is nothing but the destruction left," announces Goro.

"Asako left three days ago. She said she was going to lay flowers on her sister's grave. Does she know the location of Megumi's grave? I don't even know, and I was present for her hanging," remarks a ninja.

Goro gives out an exasperated sigh. He is sick at heart. He can't believe he has become so soft-hearted people can easily deceive him. He vows to himself he needs to get his act together and goes to his tent to sleep.

To Goro's surprise, he finds Asako the next morning coming through the front gates. She waves at Goro with a big smile. He didn't expect to see her ever again and is elated to see her return.

"Asako, I heard you went to the mountains to lay flowers on Megumi's grave. You don't even know where it is."

"It does not matter. I found a beautiful tree and placed the flowers in Megumi's name. I know her spirit is somewhere near, and that's all I needed."

Goro says, "The killers attacked two days ago. I found our weapons with our insignia on the ground. Ten men are missing from our camp. I think they were assassins, and they used my compound to hide their treachery. I hope you didn't know anything about this?"

"What? You can't believe I would be a part of something so horrendous. I left before the attack. I know it seems a coincidence that everything happened while I was gone. Why would I want to destroy the village and castle and kill all those innocent people? I have pledged my life to you, and I do not take that lightly."

"I'm sorry, Asako, I needed to be sure. When this is all over, I will take you to Megumi's site. I am the only one that knows the location. I did not want anyone to take revenge on your sister and destroy the grave."

Goro takes the ninja to help restore the village and castle. The members are angry, and they want revenge against the spies that fooled them while living in their compound. Goro tells his students they probably will never find them because they have fled far away.

It takes one year before the construction comes to completion. The old castle has new stonewalls. Everyone admires the beautiful work, and the village is back to normal. Lord Takayoshi's family is still missing. He has sent soldiers in search far and wide but to no avail. He thinks they have been killed and goes into mourning.

CHAPTER 23

Five years pass, and a message comes from the coast of Kyushu from Lord Takayoshi's old gardener Masayoshi. Masayoshi thinks Hiroko is working in a brothel nearby. He saw her walking to the marketplace and recognized her.

Lord Takayoshi is overjoyed. He doesn't care if his daughter is now a prostitute. He begins to pack for a three-week journey to the coast. Mitsujiro will be accompanying him, and Mitsujiro suggests asking Goro to join them.

It is March of 1669, and Lord Takayoshi, Mitsujiro, and Goro are sailing to the coast of Kyushu. They are dressed as commoners so as not to attract attention. Two days out, they encounter a massive storm. Three men fall into the water, and the sailors toss out ropes.

"Sharks!" Yells a sailor.

They watch as the sharks circle the men. Goro tries to distract them by shooting arrows. He finds his mark and blood comes spurting out. The sharks leave the drowning men and go directly for the thrashing fish. The crew can now rescue all the men in the treacherous water. The last man to be hauled up on deck has fainted. His color is pale, and his eyes are rolling back. He is barely alive. Two crewmembers take him below. Two hours later it is reported the man has died. He is wrapped in cloth and thrown over the side of the ship.

The weather improves, and the ship finally arrives at port. Goro questions the captain if he knows of any human trafficking of women. The captain claims he is honest and would never do such a thing. Goro says he is not accusing him but would like to know if he has heard of other ships doing the dirty deed? The captain is not forthcoming, and Goro drops the subject. He will go to an inn and try to get the information from drunken sailors.

Takayoshi goes from one teahouse to another, asking after his daughter Hiroko and his wife, Masaye. No one has any information about the two women. He thinks perhaps the women have changed their names and are in hiding.

The police tell Daimyo Takayoshi a prostitute is dead. It is a gruesome tale, and he prays the girl is not his daughter Hiroko. The murdered woman and Hiroko are the same age.

The young prostitute's throat is cut open, and she is a victim of rape. The police find her near a stall in the marketplace. She is naked, and blood is everywhere. The authorities are visiting each brothel to find out her identity. Takayoshi goes to the police station to view the body of the dead woman. He breathes a sigh of relief when he finds it is not his daughter Hiroko.

Takayoshi's old gardener does not know where Hiroko works. For three days and nights, they search the brothels for his daughter. On the fourth day, Mitsujiro bumps into a woman that recognizes him.

"Aren't you Mitsujiro? I know your sister Hatsune. Did you come to visit? Hatsune did not tell me you were in town. Don't you remember me? I used to live two houses away from you. I am Junko."

"Hatsune is here? How can I get in touch with her? I was here on business and have lost touch with her. I would like to see her very much. Can you take me to her now?"

"Of course, just follow me. Hatsune tutors the governor's daughter, and I got her the job when she first came to town. I work as a maid and know the governor was looking for a teacher for Chiyoko."

Mitsujiro is happy to learn his sister is not a prostitute. He follows Junko to a sizable gated home in a wealthy area of town. Junko enters the back door and gestures for Mitsujiro to follow. He goes through the kitchen, through a long corridor, and to a room at the back. Junko slides open the shoji door and enters.

"I have a surprise for you. Look who is here?"

Hatsune looks up and sees Mitsujiro. She jumps up and runs into his open arms. She is speechless as she hugs him.

"How did you find me? I have been in this town since the attack on the castle five years ago. Junko found me getting off a ship, holding me as a prisoner with Lord Takayoshi's wife and daughter. Junko knew the captain and had me released. I don't know what happened to Masaye and Hiroko. I have searched but never found them."

"Daimyo Takayoshi, Goro, and I have come to rescue Hiroko. We were also hoping to find you and Hiroko's mother. We think Hiroko is a prostitute. We have been searching for the brothels but cannot find her. She must be using a different name," replies Mitsujiro.

Takayoshi, Mitsujiro, and Goro take turns watching the marketplace. Finally, on the last Friday of the month, they see Hiroko at one of the stalls. She is fingering hair ribbons and holding them up to her hair. She is looking into a mirror at her reflection when she sees her father's face. She drops the ribbons and turns. Takayoshi runs to his daughter and lifts her and whirls her around. Joyful tears are running down both their faces.

"Where is your mother? Do you live together? I have been searching for you two for five years. Our former gardener, Masayoshi, said he had seen you in the marketplace and sent me a message."

"Mother is dead. She died on the ship coming here. She kept vomiting and lost a lot of weight, and when she died, they threw her into the sea. I'm sorry I could not save her. The captain kept us down in the hold with about twenty women. They gave us gruel to eat once a day. It was like dishwater. We had to use two pails as privies. The crew came down once a day to throw the waste into the water. There were no beds, and we were cramped together. If we wanted to lie down, we had to take turns. The sanitation was so inadequate many people got sick and died. I don't know how I survived."

Takayoshi nods his head and listens to his daughter's tragic story.

"Hiroko, let us go to your house and pick up your things. Mitsujiro will bring Hatsune to the harbor in two days. The ship we came on will be returning the day after tomorrow. I have already booked passage for the five of us."

"I don't think I can leave. I am ashamed to tell you, but I live in a brothel. I know you will not want me to go home with you. Sooner or later, someone you know might recognize me, and will only bring shame to you. Thank you for coming, but I am staying here," replies Hiroko adamantly.

"I will never be ashamed of you. You only wanted to survive. I am taking you home, and I don't want any more protests from you."

The return trip is calm and peaceful. The ship is riding with the wind and is nice and smooth. Lord Takayoshi rehires Hatsune, and she moves back into the castle. After one year, Lord Takayoshi asks

Hatsune to be his wife. She gives up her dream to become a nun and marries Takayoshi.

Goro is dazzled over Hiroko. He knows she is a lady of the night, but it doesn't seem to bother him. He knows his social status is beneath that of Hiroko, but he pursues her just the same. He asks Lord Takayoshi for her hand in marriage. To Goro's surprise, Lord Takayoshi is delighted with the request. They will marry in August 1670.

CHAPTER 24

Mitsuko feels a sudden foreboding and rushes to the bedchamber, and she finds Sange gasping for air. Mitsuko calls a doctor, but it is too late. Sange is fifty-one years of age and dies from heart failure.

It is August 5, 1671, and there is no cloud in the sky. The procession continues through the village led by Daimyo Takayoshi. The daimyo is atop a beautiful white stallion wearing his formal black wear.

People line up along the roadside for a glimpse of Lord Sange's coffin. The villagers drop to their knees to show respect to their beloved samurai leader. His reputation for valor is unmatched throughout Japan. Two black palanquins follow. In the first conveyance, Mitsuko rides with her children. The second palanquin holds Masako and her three children. The members of the Ouchi Clan follow the cortege on horseback. They bury Lord Sange, and everyone goes to the castle for light refreshments.

The past few days have been hectic. After Sange's death, Sange's body had to be thoroughly washed and shaved. They cut his hair and changed his clothing. They held short rites, and the immediate family had to go through a period of private mourning. The first rite was the makura service or the pillow service, which is performed right after death. The family had to change into their black mourning clothes, abstain from eating raw seafood, and refrain from working. Sange received his Buddhist name, and mourners had a communal meal to install Sange in the afterlife and to restore the mourners to the secular society.

Sange's body had been carefully put into a coffin and transferred to where the priest performed three rites while the body laid in place. The lid was closed, and the deceased likeness or painted picture stood above the altar, and a wake took place. They took the coffin to the cremation ground, where relatives sipped on hot tea. The final rite was the lighting of the funeral pyre. All these symbolic rites were for Sange as a person of the elite society.

Now the family will have to endure forty-nine days of mourning that will include offerings to smooth the way by regular memorial services and additional offerings extending at least for three years.

The passage of Sange's soul, through the critical forty-nine day period after death, will ensure he will be reborn into the Buddhist Pure Land.

CHAPTER 25

It is a rainy night in Uji, and the air is muggy. Masahiro steps outside a teahouse and hears a woman's scream in the darkness. Masahiro sees seven swordsmen rushing towards a woman. Masahiro draws his sword as he impales the chest of one. There is an ear-piercing wail as Masahiro diagonally cuts an assailant's right shoulder down to his hips. Blood is spurting everywhere, and a scream comes from the woman as a knife goes through her chest. The woman is choking on her blood as she falls to the ground. Masahiro hears running footsteps as he attacks another assassin. Help arrives, and the assailants run away. Masahiro wonders who the dead woman is and bends down to look at her face. Masahiro recognizes the courtesan but does not know her name. He wipes the blood from his sword with a piece of paper and throws it into the gutter. Masahiro slides his blade back into his sheath.

A shadow falls over Masako's face as she greets her husband. His hakama is bloodstained.

"Don't worry; it is not my blood. Assassins were accosting a woman, and I intervened. Unfortunately, she was struck and died. I don't know the reason for the attack, but I did recognize her as one of the courtesans that live nearby. She is a friend of Hiroko, the daimyo's daughter."

The following day Masahiro is perusing papers on how to commit "seppuku" properly. He finds that if one plunges his short sword into the left side of the stomach and continue to slice straight across to the right side, then cut with the tip of the sword diagonally upward, slicing across to the right nipple, death will be immediate. It also says that the samurai should dress in a white ceremonial kimono and have a second to behead him before he suffers. The samurai writes and leaves a death poem in beautiful calligraphy.

Masako finds Masahiro deep in thought. She looks down onto the papers of suicide and begins to cry. Masahiro roars with laughter and assures her he is not planning to die. She keeps trembling as he holds her. She tells him if he did commit seppuku, she will take the children and join him.

Mitsuko is on her deathbed, and her death rattle begins. The physicians give up hope for her recovery. They said she has tuberculosis. Her lungs are congested, and she is spitting up mucous mixed with blood. Masahiro sits next to her, trying to spoon tea into her mouth. The liquid dribbles down her mouth and neck. Three hours pass, and she is dead. They place Mitsuko next to Sange in the family cemetery.

Shina picks up a paper fan. The night breeze is warm, and the mosquitoes are buzzing around her neck. Her eyesight has waned, and she leans closer to the lantern to sew. Taiji comes in from the privy and gives his wife a reassuring smile. A large pot of chicken soup is stewing over a fire and quickly consumed, another day comes to a close.

Shina and Taiji come down from the mountain to visit Masako and her family. Masahiro is still mourning his mother's death. The grandchildren are rapidly growing, and they welcome their grandparents with hugs and kisses.

Taiji dies from pneumonia. He catches a cold during the winter and never recovers. Shina finds him under a tree gathering honey. The bees are buzzing around his body, covered with the fallen sweet honeycombs. Shina is overwrought, and Masako takes her home to live in Uji. After three months, Shina dies from a broken heart.

Hiroko and Goro's marriage is in ruins. Hiroko has discovered she is a carrier of syphilis—a sexual disease. During her prostitution days, many sailors had visited her brothel, and the sailors had brought the dreaded disease from abroad. Now she has passed it on to Goro, and he lies in agony as his manhood is full of pus. The doctors have inundated him with herbal medicine, but it has not helped. The physicians are helpless as he suffers. It all began with red rashes on his body and later pustules on his genitals with excruciating pain following. Now he is going blind.

"I want to die! Hiroko, you must give me something to stop the pain!"

Hiroko goes in search of the Nightshade plant. Ingesting just a few of its berries can kill an adult. She decides Goro has suffered enough. She will mash them and brew tea. Hiroko decides she will drink the tea with Goro and die with him. Two days later, they are found dead with their arms around one another.

There is a chanting throughout the castle and village. Bells are ringing in the air.

"Daimyo Takayoshi is dead. Praise Daimyo Takayoshi."

Daimyo Takayoshi and his wife Hatsune are found dead in their bedchamber. An intruder had entered the castle and killed them while asleep. Mitsujiro discovers them when he returns from a stroll on the castle grounds.

"I think the daimyo tried to protect his wife. His blade is out, but he did not have time to use it. Hatsune is under him as the intruder's blade went through both their bodies. They died instantly."

Mitsujiro informs Lord Masahiro about the murder of Daimyo Takayoshi. Masahiro travels to meet with the shogun to tell him of the death. The shogun is shocked, but there is nothing he can do. He says he will send out soldiers to find the assassin, but he believes there is little chance to find them. He decides to elevate Lord Masahiro to the daimyo position. Masahiro is speechless as he accepts the high honour. He returns home and tells Masako that he is now the new daimyo. She congratulates her husband and tells him he deserves the honour. She calls out to their children to come and celebrate their father's new position. The villagers come to greet their new leader.

"Banzai! Banzai!" echoes through the streets.

The ceremony to become one of the top-ranking men of Japan begins. Masahiro dresses in a dark black kimono. The colour black signifies the most powerful. After the black kimono come the colours of red, green, and finally purple to complete his wardrobe, and his primary duty is to protect the shoguns. He will be the ruler of his people, land, and properties of his assigned areas. He will provide military support and samurai and live in a castle. He will move his family to Daimyo Takayoshi's castle, away from the village of Uji.

Masako is not too thrilled to be in this new lifestyle. Her husband will have the power to control how much taxes the farmers, craftsmen, merchants, and villagers will have to pay. Masahiro will have to give his finest samurai, rice, and lands to the shogun to show his loyalty. Masahiro will be required to pay a portion of their taxable earnings to the Bukufu and must live in Edo for part of the year. The Bukufu is the military government headed by the shogun. She knows Masahiro cannot refuse the orders of the shogun that elevated him to be the new daimyo. Her husband is now thirty-two years old in September of 1671.

CHAPTER 26

In August of 1672, there is a severe drought, and it hasn't rained for forty days and nights. All the rice fields are drying up, and people are starving. Masahiro goes to the Shinto shrine to pray for rain. He goes to the Buddhist temple in Mt. Koya and prays. Masahiro sends a request throughout the region for everyone to pray and conserve water. The farmers try to dig additional wells, but they find the earth dried up. Elderly people are dying, and newborns cannot survive.

Masahiro has responsibilities to keep his subjects healthy and well. He decides he must empty his coffers of rice and save his people.

Masahiro sends his army onto the mountain to divert the waterfall to the valley below. The usual abundant falls are just a small trickle. Because there is no recourse, he orders the soldiers to dig ditches from the falls to the rice fields below. They split the large bamboo stalks in half and use it to run the water down to the rice fields. He hopes somehow water can be diverted and used by both the farmers and villagers. This solution helps for a month, but slowly, the small trickle completely disappears.

Masako is down by the riverbed, trying to fill buckets with water. She fills up the wooden kegs and has the soldiers take them into the village to disperse. She prays for rain, but the cloudless sky above is clear.

It is October when the rain finally falls. People are ecstatic, and they stand under the drops, getting soaked to the skin. Masahiro orders the soldiers to fill large barrels with the rainwater. He tells the villagers and farmers to gather up all the raindrops in containers. People are rejoicing as they revel in the falling rain.

Masahiro decides to build large wooden tubs. The tubs will be suspended high above the ground to gather rain or snow. When they are full, they will be covered so the water will not evaporate. Masahiro doesn't ever want to go through another drought.

Masako finds her son Yoshiaki helping the soldiers pass out baskets of rice. He is fifteen years old and tall at five feet eight. He is in training to become a samurai warrior like his ancestors before him.

Yoshiaki is very kind and treats all the servants and villagers with respect. He is always smiling and willing to help wherever and whoever needs it. Everyone says he would take the shirt off his back to help someone.

Kazuo and Midori are Yoshiaki's younger siblings, and the twins are thirteen years old. They are always running after their older brother and pestering him. Yoshiaki just laughs and doesn't seem to mind. He watches over the twins and makes sure no harm comes to them.

Masahiro helps to train Yoshiaki with his kendo lessons. He can see his son is going to be a great warrior. His agility and strength will surpass his ancestors.

December brings a substantial snowstorm. Icicles hang dangerously from the eaves of the houses. The guards are standing in front of blazing fires trying to keep warm. Inside the castle, the maids are warming the beds with pans filled with hot coals. The children have taken a bath and are now eating a hot meal. Masako will tell them a bedtime story before they are in dreamland.

Masako feels a sudden movement. She glances up, alarmed. The room is shifting, and things are falling. She leaps up and gathers her children. She leads them to a safer place inside the castle walls. Masahiro comes running and tells her it is an earthquake. The quake lasts for about a minute and stops. The younger two children are in tears, and they reach for their father's arms. Yoshiaki is being brave and doesn't show his anxiety. The maids and guards make sure the family is unhurt. Everyone goes back to what they were doing before the world was falling apart.

Masahiro sends out soldiers to assess the damage in the village.

The earthquake has not caused much destruction. A few stones come loose from the top of the castle walls. The village is intact except for a small fire when a piece of burning wood fell onto a nearby thatched roof.

New Year's Day is just a week away. The year 1671, is almost over, and the year 1672, will soon begin.

CHAPTER 27

An elderly woman comes knocking at the castle gate. She wears a brown kimono and a dark brown obi. The woman is thin, and her skin is wrinkled. She is at least seventy if not eighty.

Masako greets the woman, "*Konichi-wa*, good day. What can I do for you?"

The woman looks surprised as she glances at Masako's face.

"My name is Kishi. I was the midwife that delivered you and your sister. Your father was Emperor Morihito, and your mother was Empress Kanaye. You look just like Princess Natsuye. You are Princess Akiko, are you not?"

Masako is startled. She doesn't know if she should reveal her true identity. She wonders what this woman wants and if she is here to harm?

The woman continues with her story, "No one knows about Natsuye's birth because I stole her away as soon as she was born. It was a bad omen to birth twins, and they usually killed the younger baby. I could not kill Natsuye, so my assistant hid her. I have no ulterior motive. I just want you and your sister to meet."

Masako is speechless. Did she have a twin? She wants to confer with her husband and excuses herself. She finds Masahiro in the garden pruning a bonsai plant, and Masako tells Masahiro about the woman named Kishi. Masahiro says he would like to meet Kishi and follows Masako back to the tatami room.

Masako reveals that she is Princess Akiko, and she tells Kishi she wants to meet her twin sister. The elderly woman says Natsuye is at a nearby inn, and she will bring Natsuye the following day. Masako agrees to meet for tea at two in the afternoon.

Masako cannot sleep. She is nervous and restless. She is excited to meet her twin, but she is also apprehensive. She rises at dawn and paces around the garden. Finally, it is almost two, and she asks the maid to bring in refreshments.

The maid brings Kishi and Natsuye into the garden. Masako is stunned when she sees her twin sister. Natsuye is a mirror image of herself, and Masako can't believe it! Masahiro's mouth gapes open when he sees his wife's twin.

Masahiro says, "If I didn't know you were Natsuye, I would swear you were my wife. I am happy to meet you, and you are welcome in my home. If you would like to stay in the castle, you can, and I'm sure my wife feels the same way?"

Masako doesn't know if she wants Natsuye to stay with them. She feels a sudden unwelcoming feeling about her sister. There is a coldness in her demeanor, and her smile does not seem to come from her heart.

Masako says, "Of course you are both welcome to stay with us for a few days. You have come on a long journey and must be exhausted. It will be wonderful to talk to you both, and I'm sure you will want to go back home as soon as possible. I can come and visit you now and then."

When the Nightingale Sings

Both Kishi and Natsuye feel the hesitation in Masako's tone. Masako is making it clear she does not want either one staying for an extended period. Kishi is disappointed because Kishi thought they had a place to live for the rest of their lives. Both she and Natsuye are almost out of money and have nowhere to go. Kishi decides if they move in, they can make excuses and extend their visit indefinitely.

"*Domo arigato gozaimasu.* We will stay for a few days if you don't mind. I'm sorry we do not have any gifts for your family. We did not know if we would find Natsuye's twin. If you could show us our rooms, we can settle in. What time is the evening meal?"

Masako is angry, and she tells Masahiro that Kishi and Natsuye lack in manners. Although Natsuye is her twin, she does not find her to be warm and friendly. Masako doesn't like either one of the women. Masahiro can't understand why Masako is not welcoming. His wife is usually kind.

Natsuye is pulling one dress after another out of her bag. She doesn't have many kimonos, and she is not pleased. Natsuye selects an old faded lavender kimono and opens the bedroom door and peeks out. There is no one about, and Natsuye rushes to Masako's bedchamber.

Masahiro is in the bathhouse soaking in the tub. He hears a creak outside the door, and suddenly, it opens. Masahiro is surprised to see his wife entering. She has a towel around her body, and she is naked as she approaches with a smile on her face. She takes off her towel and begins to scrub her body. Masahiro watches as he becomes aroused. She rinses the soap off her body and steps into the ofuro. Masako has never done something like this before, and Masahiro is stunned. Before he can say anything, she grabs him and kisses him. Masahiro returns the kiss and begins to knead her breasts. Masahiro moans as she rubs her body against him and strokes. Suddenly she stands and lets him take in her naked body. She turns, and Masahiro is shocked. She is not his wife, and there is no heart-shaped blue birthmark on her buttocks. Masahiro was almost unfaithful to his wife, and

Masahiro decides not to tell Masako about this incident because it will only hurt her.

Masahiro shouts, "Natsuye, I know you are not my wife. Why are you doing this? Leave now before I tell Masako. I will keep this a secret for now, but if you ever do something like this again, I promise you will live to regret it. Get out of my sight, and don't ever come near me again."

It is over one month, and Kishi and Natsuye are still living in the castle. They seem to come up with excuse after excuse to stay, and Masako is trying her best to keep her temper. Finally, Masako decides the two women must go.

Masako says, "It has been wonderful having both of you visiting. I'm sorry, but it is time for you to go. We are having guests coming to stay, and we need all our bedchambers. You will have to leave by the beginning of next week, and that should give you enough time to pack and make your travel plans. Please tell me the place of your residence so I can get in touch with you at a later time."

Masako tells Masahiro that she told her guests to leave by the beginning of the week. Masahiro nods his head in agreement. He did not tell Masako about the bathhouse episode. Masahiro feels guilty, but he thinks it is best to leave it unsaid.

"My lady, I can't find the gold kanzashi you wanted to wear for the party next week, and I have looked everywhere. Do you remember when you wore it last? I know it is expensive, and I am worried," explains the maid.

"I wore the hairpin during the New Year's festivities, and I know I put it back into the jewelry chest. I hope Midori wasn't playing in my room and took it out. I will have to question her when she comes back from her lessons," replies Masako.

The maid tells Midori her mother's hairpin is missing, and Midori swears she did not touch the kanzashi. Masako knows her daughter never lies and would say to her if she had lost it. Masako becomes suspicious and wonders if one of her guests borrowed it or stole it. Masako asks the maid to come to her room and check to see if anything else is missing.

Nori checks through Masako's expensive clothes and finds one blue-silk kimono and the matching obi missing. Masako asks Nori to search through Kishi and Natsuye's belongings when they leave to take a bath.

The maid rushes into Masako's bedchamber and shows her the missing clothes and hairpin. Nori says she found them in Natsuye's room under her futon. Masako is enraged, and she waits in Natsuye's bedchamber until she returns from the bath. Masako confronts her twin and tells Natsuye to leave immediately, or she will have a guard toss her out. Kishi hears the loud voices and comes into the room. She looks at Natsuye and shakes her head. Kishi knows she will have to leave. There are no more excuses, and Kishi feels hopeless and forlorn.

Masahiro does not wish the two women a safe journey, and he watches them leave from a balcony on the far side of the castle. Masahiro is glad they are going. Masako was right when she said they did not belong. Masahiro prays Masako never finds out about his almost indiscretion.

CHAPTER 28

Kazuo's hair is in a topknot, and he looks like a proud samurai warrior of the Ouchi Clan. Kazuo, however, has other dreams of becoming a doctor. He knows his parents will not be happy if he does not follow in the footsteps of his ancestors. In the meantime, Kazuo emulates his brother to keep the peace. Yoshiaki has earned many medals and is well-known throughout the samurai clans of Japan.

Midori is fifteen, beautiful, and elegant. Midori is sitting near a lake in the meadow wearing a silk aquamarine coloured kimono and a red obi sash. She looks up as her twin brother approaches. Kazuo has come to take her home.

Midori notices that Kazuo is not alone, and Kazuo's samurai friend Kentaro is standing behind him. Midori shyly smiles and greets Kentaro. Kentaro is handsome in his navy kimono and sky-blue obi sash as he peers around Kazuo and grins.

Kazuo says, "I have invited Kentaro for dinner. He is an excellent mathematician, and I need his expertise. We are planning some strategic maneuvers, and Kentaro's ideas are invaluable."

During dinner, Kentaro keeps glancing at Midori, and feels a pull on his heartstrings, and can't seem to look away. Midori sits with her eyes downcast and feels Kentaro's eyes boring into her. Midori feels happiness run through her body, and she looks up as Kentaro, and her eyes meet. Midori's face turns red, and she looks away.

The following day Kentaro's father, Lord Satoshi, comes to the castle bearing gifts. Lord Satoshi asks to see Daimyo Masahiro and his wife, Masako. Lord Satoshi is seated in the tatami room with a cup of tea when Masahiro and Masako appear. Lord Satoshi quickly rises, and bows and Masahiro and Masako bow back respectfully.

"*Ohayo gozaimasu*, good morning. Thank you for receiving me. I have come at the request of my son Kentaro. My son would like to marry your daughter if she will have him? Kentaro has been admiring Midori-sama from afar and has fallen deeply in love with her beauty and gentleness. I have brought a few gifts. Please accept them."

There are five gifts wrapped in a furoshiki. There is a bolt of white brocade, a beautiful gold-threaded obi, a gold kanzashi, and two gifts of dried foods.

Masako bows low as she accepts the gifts and thanks Lord Satoshi for his generosity. Lord Satoshi returns her bow respectfully.

"Thank you for asking for my daughter's hand in marriage. It is an honour to have such an auspicious samurai family wanting to have Midori for a daughter-in-law. Masako and I have always wanted our children to have love matches and choose their mates. I hope you do not think ill of our family, but we would like to discuss this marriage with Midori. If Midori is willing, and I think she will be, we can set a wedding date when we next meet. Would that be all right with you, your wife, and son?" asks Masahiro imploringly.

Lord Satoshi bows and says he understands. He says he hopes the answer will be positive, and the wedding plans can move forward. Lord Satoshi steps into his palanquin and departs.

All is well. Midori is more than willing to marry Kentaro, and they set their wedding for the spring of 1673.

Kentaro courts Midori for months. He is attentive and gentle, and Midori falls deeply in love.

Midori's wedding day is here. Following tradition, the Shinto ceremony will take place at Kentaro's home. Arriving at her groom's house, she changes into a beautiful bridal kimono given to her by Kentaro's family. Midori is floating on air—a happy bride. The wedding guests arrive, and the breeze is heavy with the perfume of the floral arrangements.

Midori and Kentaro sit in front of the altar. Kentaro wears a black silk kimono with imprints of five family crests. Beneath his kimono, Kentaro is wearing a wide black-and-white striped hakama. The Shinto priest begins to chant. Towards the end of the ceremony, Midori reaches for a cup filled with sake, extending from the priest's hand. She touches the cup to her lips three times and gives it to Kentaro. The second and third cups pass in the same way, and the wedding is at an end, and the marriage sealed.

The wedding night approaches. Midori bathes and waits in anticipation for Kentaro to come to their bedchamber. She hears his footsteps outside the door and crawls under the futon. The shoji door slides open, and suddenly, Midori sees Kentaro's bare feet. Midori looks up and sees a strange look on her husband's face. Midori feels a little frightened, but when Kentaro smiles, she relaxes.

Kentaro pulls off the comforter and roughly rips off Midori's silk robe. Midori can smell the liquor on his breath and tries to push Kentaro away, but he is too strong. Kentaro's face contorts, and his leering look scares Midori to the core. Kentaro pushes Midori down and is on top of her in a blinking of an eye. Kentaro pulls her mouth up to his for a hard-punishing kiss. Midori tries to pull herself away as she feels dizzy and disoriented. Midori is sobbing as she takes in a shaky breath.

"Be quiet, or I will kill you."

Kentaro pulls out his swollen membrane and rubs it along her quivering thighs. Kentaro is breathing faster, and Midori lets out a small muffled groan.

Kentaro slaps Midori, holds her hands above her body, and spreads her legs apart. He pushes into Midori without any warning. Midori tries to scream, but Kentaro's left hand is pushing against her throat—choking her. Kentaro begins to move, and Midori feels pain as he breaks through her maidenhead. Midori tosses her head from side to side in protest. A low groan comes from Kentaro's throat as he climaxes. Kentaro releases Midori and falls asleep.

Midori is so frightened she can't stop shaking. She crawls out of bed and tries to stand, but her legs are like rubber. Suddenly Kentaro has her by the hair and pulls her down. Midori whimpers and feels like a rag doll. Kentaro enters Midori from the back and laughs as he rides her. Midori begins to cry. She rubs her sore head, and gobs of loose hair fall into her hands. Kentaro turns over and falls back asleep.

Midori is sobbing uncontrollably and goes to the washbowl in the corner of the room. She uses the lukewarm water and a small hand towel to wash. Midori scrubs so hard it is painful, and Midori is in a frenzy trying to rid herself of Kentaro's scent and bloody sticky sperm.

Midori quickly dresses and rushes out of the room. She runs down the long corridor and runs into one of the maids. The maid looks surprised to see Midori and asks if everything is all right? Midori asks the maid to get one of the guards to take her to the castle. A guard puts her into a palanquin, and within one hour, the palanquin stops, and Midori leaps out and runs through the entryway into her parent's bedchamber.

"Please help me! Kentaro just attacked me. I am so frightened, and I don't ever want to see him again."

Masako and Masahiro stare at their daughter in disbelief. Midori keeps telling them Kentaro hurt her. Masako tries to tell Midori sex can be painful the first time. Masako lights a candle and looks into Midori's eyes. She sees the imprint of a hand on her throat and a red mark across her right cheek. Midori's hands have scratches, and her lips cut. Masako gasps as she comprehends the rape of her daughter. Masahiro quickly dresses and grabs his sword to seek out Kentaro and make him pay. Masako looks at her husband's murderous face and tries to stop him. Masako calls out for Yoshiaki and Kazuo to stop their father from committing murder. Masako quickly explains what has taken place, and Yoshiaki and Kazuo swiftly go to the stable to get their horses. Their father is already gone, and the stable master says he is in a rage.

Forty-five minutes later, they see their father at the gate of Kentaro's house. The guard recognizes his daimyo and bows and opens the gate, and Masahiro rushes through. Yoshiaki and Kazuo arrive just as the guard closes the gate. Yoshiaki tells the guard if he does not immediately open the gate, he will kill him. Kazuo draws his sword ready to strike, and the guard trembles as he opens the entryway.

Yoshiaki and Kazuo gallop through the open gate. It is going to take some time before they can find their father and Kentaro. The two men dismount and dash into the house. Yoshiaki and Kazuo can hear the running footsteps of their father as he searches for Kentaro's bedchamber. Suddenly the entire household seems to be awake, and maids and soldiers are running about thinking an intruder has entered. The brothers intercept Lord Satoshi with a sword in his hand, and Lord Satoshi halts as he encounters Midori's brothers.

"What is happening? Why are you two here? We thought an intruder had entered. I will tell the soldiers to leave, and I apologize for making a mistake. It would have been better if you informed us you were coming, so we would have avoided this entire fiasco and this embarrassment," replies Lord Satoshi.

"We are here to talk to your son Kentaro so please lead us to his bedchamber. My father is already here searching for his room. Your son raped my sister last night, and Midori is recuperating at home," explains Yoshiaki angrily.

"What? You must have misunderstood. My son would never do such a thing, and Kentaro is a very loving and gentle person. Why would your sister lie? I don't understand."

"Just lead us to your son's bedchamber, and we will sort this out after we talk to Kentaro. We best hurry before my father kills him. My father is so mad it will be hard to stop him from hurting your son. I understand my father's grief and anger as I am trying to hold back my rage as well. I thought Kentaro was my friend. I'm sorry I introduced my sister to such an evil person," shouts Kazuo.

Lord Satoshi, Yoshiaki, and Kazuo find Kentaro trembling under Masahiro's sword. Kentaro is begging for his life as Masahiro raises his sword to strike. Kentaro's mother, Sada, runs into the room, and she lies on top of her son to protect him. Lord Satoshi is glued to the floor, unable to move. Everything seems to be moving in slow motion as Yoshiaki removes the sword from his father's hand.

"No, father. He is not worth it. He is not even a human being. Let's go home and let Lord Satoshi deal with his son, and even animals are more humane than this bastard. Kentaro will never be a samurai in the Ouchi Clan, and I will make certain he resigns for personal reasons. Kentaro, you better agree, or I will kill you myself," whispers Yoshiaki.

Kentaro's father cannot believe his son has committed rape. Kentaro was always a kind and considerate child, and Lord Satoshi cannot understand what possessed Kentaro to rape Midori. Lord Satoshi decides he must apologize to Daimyo Masahiro's family and rides to their castle.

Lord Satoshi arrives in the early afternoon and asks the guard to announce his presence. He watches Daimyo Masahiro storm towards the front gate.

"How dare you come to the castle? Your presence is not welcome. Kentaro has done enough damage, and I am going to vanquish him to some remote area. Your family's honour broke, and you are in disgrace. Shogun Morimatsu is removing your family from our samurai clan. Your son has not taken any responsibility for his behavior, nor has Kentaro apologized."

Lord Satoshi is kneeling as he begs, "Please accept my humble apologies. There is nothing I can say to remedy this horrible attack on your daughter. I never thought my son was capable of such a heinous act. Kentaro has always been a loving and kind son, and I cannot comprehend how he could have violated Midori-san in such a cruel way. I will get to the bottom of this terrible crime, and I assure you Kentaro will suffer my wrath ten-fold. Moushiwake gozaimasen deshita, I am deeply sorry."

Masahiro turns as Masako comes running out. She is crying, and tears are flowing down her cheeks.

"Please leave. Your son has done enough damage. You are not welcome here, and I never want to see you or your family again. Your apology is falling on deaf ears, so you might as well go home. I thought I was a warm and forgiving person, but your son has proven me wrong. I will never forgive Kentaro as long as I live. My poor daughter is troubled and suffering because of Kentaro's cruel act. Go home and tell your son he is not even a human being."

Yoshiaki suddenly appears and comes to lead his mother away.

"Oka-san, Mother, please let's go back inside. Lord Satoshi is only making you angrier, and you need to get some rest and eat. You are making yourself sick, and we need you to be strong for Midori's sake."

"Masako, get back into the castle. You do not have to endure seeing Lord Satoshi. He has come to apologize, but it will not be accepted. If it were my son, I would demand him to commit seppuku. He has dishonoured our daughter, and Kentaro deserves to be dead," responds Masahiro in anger.

Lord Satoshi is on the ground, sobbing and apologizing over and over as the next day approaches. In the early morning, the guard knocks on the castle door and informs the maid that Lord Satoshi is still at the gate and has not left. The sentry wants to know what to do.

Masahiro tells the guard to ignore Lord Satoshi. If Lord Satoshi wants to sit out in front of the castle gates, so be it! Lord Satoshi finally leaves after three days since there is nothing more he can do. They do not accept his apology, and he decides to go home. Lord Satoshi can barely stand as he mounts his horse. His head is hanging in shame, and the guard feels pity for Lord Satoshi as he rides away.

Lord Satoshi arrives home in the early dawn. He looks in on his wife and children, and they are all asleep. Lord Satoshi asks the maid for a light supper and a bottle of sake. He takes a hot bath and dresses in a white kimono. The lord cuts off his topknot with a short knife called a tanto. Lord Satoshi goes to his desk and begins to write a short poem.

"FAREWELL
I PASS AS ALL THINGS DO
FOG IN THE AIR"

Lord Satoshi goes out to his beloved garden and takes a stroll. He stoops down and watches the golden koi swimming and listens to a frog croaking. He plucks a red rose and accidentally punctures his finger with a thorn. Lord Satoshi looks at the blood and begins to laugh as though crazed. He sits down on the ground and gives a short prayer. Lord Satoshi wraps a white cloth around his forehead and hair. He opens his kimono and picks up his short sword. Lord Satoshi stabs himself in the belly, slices open his stomach and turns the blade upward to ensure a fatal wound.

In the morning, a passing maid screams.

"Help, the master is dead. He has committed hara-kiri."

Sada and her children rush into the garden and see Lord Satoshi with his intestines spilling out of his body. Sada begins to wail and runs to her husband's side. Sada looks crazed as she tries to push her husband's intestines back inside his stomach. Blood covers Sada's hands.

Kentaro turns pale and begins to vomit, and the other children turn away in shock. Sada goes to Kentaro and slaps him across the face.

"Look what you have caused. Because of your evil deed, I have lost a good husband, and your siblings have lost a loving father. Our family is disgraced, and you should be the one dead and not your father. Your father died in your place because you are a coward. I want you out of this house immediately, and I don't want to know where you go, and I don't care."

Kentaro hangs his head and leaves.

A week goes by, and a message arrives for Masahiro. It comes from Lord Satoshi's wife, Sada.

She apologies for her son's rape, and notifies Masahiro that her husband committed seppuku, the moment he arrived home from the castle. Masahiro and Masako are stunned, and send a letter of condolence to the widow. Masahiro and Masako want to let Sada know they do not blame her in any way.

Sada takes to her bed with her husband's death; she doesn't know how to handle his funeral service. Lord Satoshi's body is lying in front of their Buddhist altar. She has a servant go to a nearby temple to ask one of the monks to come to perform a service. Because Lord Satoshi is no longer a member of the Ouchi Clan, he cannot have a samurai funeral. She cremates Lord Satoshi's body and takes his ashes to the Mt Koya Buddhist temple. She asks the abbot to care for the ashes and leaves a sizable donation.

Masahiro orders his soldiers to take Kentaro to a remote area to live out the rest of his life in shame. His family has disowned him, and he will be exiled alone. Sada decides to move to another prefecture, to start a new life, where they will be unknown.

Midori has nightmares nightly and can't get Kentaro's brutal attacks out of her mind. She is sick to her stomach and seems to redraw from reality. A physician discovers that Midori is pregnant. She wants to abort the baby, but Masako talks her out of it. She tells Midori the baby is innocent and should not kill the baby because of the father's horrible deed.

The baby girl is born healthy in December of 1673, and Midori names her Sayori. Kentaro and his family are forbidden to see the new baby. Midori is slowly recovering from her depression and finding solace with Sayori's birth. Midori looks in on her sleeping daughter to find Sayori has kicked off her futon. Midori covers the baby and returns to her bed alone.

Sayori is turning into a wicked child, and she teases the younger neighborhood children and makes them cry. Sayori takes away the neighborhood children's toys and hides them in the garden shed. The gardener returns the stolen toys to Midori several times a week.

People think Sayori is the perfect child because she smiles and shows respect to all the elders. Sayori is going to be a rare beauty when she grows up. At eight years old, Sayori's black hair is silky, and her eyes bright and sparkly. Sayori turns the heads of many men even at her young age. Midori has given everything to Sayori and spoiled her. Midori never disciplines her and pretends everything is all right. Sayori knows how to twist her mother's will with a pouting look.

Midori finds a dead, mutilated cat in the back corridor. Midori calls a maid to have the dead cat taken away and doesn't even investigate how the dead cat got there in the first place. Midori is in denial, and the servants are whispering behind her back.

"What should we do? I don't think the mistress cares about Sayori's grotesque antics. One day Sayori is going to do something horrible. We should stay away as far as possible from that child," whispers the maid.

The two servants scurry down the hallway shaking their heads.

Masako and Masahiro come to visit. They see Sayori in the garden and are about to call out when Masako gasps. Sayori pulls a koi out of the pond and laughs as the fish flops around on the ground. The grandparents are appalled as Sayori catches a butterfly and tears it's wings apart.

"What is wrong with her? Why is she killing everything?"

"Not only is she killing everything, but Sayori is doing it cruelly," responds Masahiro.

"Where is Midori? We must get help for Sayori right away. She is only eight years old and already out of control. We can't let Sayori keep in this destructive way, or she will one day become a murderer of human life."

Masako calls out to her granddaughter, "Sayori-chan, we have come to visit you, and I have brought your favorite rice cakes."

Sayori comes running and hugs her grandparents and sweetly smiles. Masako and Masahiro do not divulge what they witnessed a few minutes ago. The grandparents stare at Sayori and wonder if Midori knows about her daughter's destructive nature? They hope not.

"Midori, where are you? Come and have some tea and rice cakes. We are in the garden with Sayori."

Midori comes rushing into the garden and claps her hands, and a maid appears. Masako hands her the furoshiki, holding the rice cakes and orders tea.

Masahiro tells Midori he wants to speak to her, and Masako says she will keep Sayori company. Masahiro leads Midori further into the garden for privacy. Midori is looking at her father with an odd look.

"What is it, Father? Is Mother ill? Or are you ill? You look so serious you are scaring me."

"Midori, we saw Sayori doing some cruel things when we arrived. She was in the garden and killed a carp and a butterfly. Your daughter took one of the koi out of the water and watched it flop around, and she was laughing. After that, Sayori pulled the wings off a butterfly. That is not ordinary behavior, and Sayori needs counseling immediately."

"Father, do not be mad. Sayori is just a little girl and doesn't know better, and I will explain to make sure Sayori understands. Now let's go back and have some of mother's delicious mochi cakes."

Masako goes to the kitchen to retrieve her furoshiki. The maids are whispering about Sayori, and they stop conversing when they see Masako.

"I heard you were speaking about my granddaughter, and I would like you to give me an honest answer. I saw her kill a koi and a butterfly in the garden. She did not know I was there, and I want to know if Sayori has done other bad things? Sayori needs help, and Midori is oblivious to Sayori's antics. Midori thinks everything Sayori does is normal. Please tell me everything I should know."

The maids glance at one another and are silent. Masako tells them they will not get into trouble if they confess. Masako will not tell Midori where she got the information, and only tell Midori what she saw in the garden.

"There was a dead cat yesterday, and the cat was almost bald without much hair. We did not see who did it, so we can't say it was your granddaughter. We do suspect her, but we have no proof. She has been teasing and bullying the younger children that live nearby. She takes their toys away and hides them in the gardener's shed. Osamu has returned the toys to the mistress, but she doesn't seem to care or scold Sayori. Midori just laughs and says Sayori is only a child and is just playing. To tell you the truth, I am scared of Sayori and keep away from her as much as possible. Sayori is a very destructive child, and we shudder to think about what type of woman she will be in a few more years. I hope you can help her?"

Masahiro tells Masako they must keep a close eye on Sayori. He is worried that if she doesn't get help, she will either hurt herself or others, and it will be too late. He thinks talking to Midori will not help, and she seems to be in another world. Masahiro thinks Midori never recovered from the brutal attack by Kentaro on their wedding night.

Masahiro goes to Mt Koya to confer with the abbot and tells the holy man all about his granddaughter. Masahiro asks if there is hope for Sayori and where she can go for treatments? The abbot tells Masahiro to bring both Midori and Sayori to the temple. He says he will pray and oversee their mental health.

Midori is thrilled to be going to Mt Koya and tells Sayori they are going on an exciting trip. Masahiro will be taking them, and Masako is busy helping the maids pack their belongings. Sayori wants to know how long they will be away. Masahiro tells Sayori he doesn't know. Sayori begins to pout but finds that little ploy will not work on her grandfather.

Masahiro thanks the abbot for taking Midori and Sayori into his care. He tells the abbot to send a message to him in case of any emergency, and he will come immediately.

Midori and Sayori fall into a daily regimen. They rise at five in the morning and go for prays. Breakfast is at six. All the meals are vegetarian foods, and Sayori is not happy and pouts and refuses to eat. The monks smile and take away her plates and leave Sayori hungry. Sayori soon learns if she doesn't eat—she will not eat at all.

The monks are Sayori's teachers, and she has classes from eight to noon. Sayori eats her lunch and goes to the temple for more prayers. The monks find Sayori to be very intelligent and praise her for being such a bright student. Sayori is still somewhat rebellious but better than when she first came. Midori is busy helping with sewing and cooking. At first, the abbot thought Midori would rebel and say she is the daimyo's daughter and would not do menial work. Midori surprises him and fits right in.

In the afternoon, the monks take Midori and Sayori into the forest to dig for roots and bring back herbs. They teach Midori and Sayori how to dry the herbs to made medicine. The two women learn which plants are poisonous, and Sayori seems to be most interested in the toxic vegetation.

The abbot makes a special bathhouse and an outhouse for Midori and Sayori. He cannot very well have them take a bath or use the same privy with the monks. The abbot insists Midori and Sayori wear simple kimono rather than the silk in their suitcases. The abbot tells the two women in Mt. Koya, there is no class distinction, and everyone is equal. Sayori is not happy that she cannot wear her silk kimono, but she relents.

After dinner and evening prayers, it is time to retire. Sayori falls asleep, and Midori reads by candlelight.

The abbot takes Sayori to the stables to see a new foal. She is excited because the abbot says she can name the new filly. Sayori's mind fills with names, and she decides the name should be Hoshi. The filly has a white spot on her forehead that looks like a star. Sayori goes to see Hoshi every morning feeding him carrots or an apple. The monks keep an eye on Sayori because they know she has hurt other living things before coming to their temple. They don't want any harm to come to their new horse.

The monks are teaching Sayori that all living things are sacred. They show her how to catch a spider with her hands and release it outdoors. A month after Sayori arrives, the abbot gives her a small puppy. The fur is short and dense, and the colour white and golden brown. The abbot tells Sayori the dog is an Akita from northern Japan, and it is a female dog, and the abbot tells Sayori to give the dog a name. She names the dog Machiko, and Sayori is learning the meaning of love and adores both the horse and puppy.

It has been one year since Midori and Sayori have come to live at the abbey, and the abbot feels it is time for them to return home. Both the women have grown to love the monks and will miss them dearly. Sayori is a changed person and is now loving and kind. Sayori treats everyone with respect, and her entire demeanor has changed. Midori feels proud of her daughter and thanks the abbot for his help.

Sayori goes to the stables to say goodbye to Hoshi. She rubs the horse's forehead, and gives Hoshi an apple, and hugs him tightly as tears run down her cheeks. Sayori hears her grandfather's voice and knows it is time to leave. Sayori kisses the horse and runs out of the barn.

Masahiro is thanking the abbot and handing him a bag of coins as a donation. The abbot bows and gives thanks. The abbot says goodbye to both Midori and Sayori and wishes them well. The abbot bends down to pet Machiko on her head and tells Sayori the dog is hers to take down the mountain. Sayori bows and thanks the abbot for his generosity. Sayori sees all the monks lining up in a row behind the abbot. The monks have grown to love the two females and have come to bid them farewell.

CHAPTER 29

Masahiro reigns as the daimyo until 1683, and Masahiro is forty-four years old when he dies from pneumonia. Masako dotes on her grandchildren and outlives Masahiro by two years and dies from a bleeding ulcer.

Masahiro and Masako's son, Yoshiaki, marries a beautiful girl named Nobuko. She comes from a samurai clan in Hiroshima prefecture, and they have three sons: Sumio, Noboru, and Kazukiyo. Yoshiaki becomes the new daimyo when Masahiro passes away. Yoshiaki is a beloved leader and a skilled swordsman, and Yoshiaki is known for being a compassionate ruler.

Masahiro's second son Kazuo becomes a physician. Kazuo always shied away from becoming a samurai warrior, and if ever Kazuo changes his mind, he is well trained and can be a warrior at any time. Kazuo marries Yoriko, who comes from the Ouchi Clan, and the couple has two children. Kazuo and Yoriko name their son Taiji after his great-grandfather, and they name their daughter Emiko.

Kazuo is interested in learning the art of acupuncture and herbal medicine. Acupuncture arrived in Japan in the fifth century from China and Korea. The two countries educated the Japanese in both acupuncture and herbal medicine. In the seventh century, the Japanese government sends scholars and priests to study Chinese culture.

Acupuncture is a common practice in the courts of the feudal lords and Buddhist temples. It is an incorporation of folk medicine and the study of the classics and techniques of ancient China.

The acupuncture needle punctures the skin, and at the end of the needle, they place a small cigar-shaped piece of burning moxa or mugwort. The needle stimulates the acupuncture points of the body and warms them. It brings good circulation and proper blood flow throughout the body and its organs.

Kazuo goes to China to study herbal medicine, and upon his return, goes to Mt Koya and studies with the monks. Kazuo learns how to dry the vegetation and distinguish which ones are poisonous. In his medicine cabinet, Kazuo keeps some poisonous herbs to counteract the poison from venomous snakebites. Kazuo is becoming renowned throughout Japan, and many people come to seek a cure for their maladies.

Midori never remarries after her ordeal with her first husband. She has many proposals of marriage, but she refuses them all. She raises her daughter Sayori with love and care. Sayori endures many trials, but the year in Mt Koya saved her life.

EPILOGUE

The Kumakura Period began in 1192, during the reign of the Kumakura Shogunate. The Mongol Kublai Khan's attempts of sea-invasions in 1274, and 1281, was unsuccessful. The Mongol fleets were blown back by a typhoon, and this act of nature was called the divine winds or kamikaze. The Japanese believed the Gods sent the winds to protect Japan.

People think Japan is a very formal, polite type of society, but the Japanese feudal period was not. The rule of Japan by regional families and clans, as well as by the shogun called warlords, created a different type of culture. There was a decrease in the power of the emperor and the ruling class.

There were a few female samurai, and they were highly valued because they showed a strong will of loyalty and bravery. The husbands of these women were usually warriors.

Male samurai were required to fight in battle, and this was a rare event for women samurai. The primary role of samurai women was to protect the home. The females managed the servants, crops, food supplies, children, as well as being responsible for the duty of revenge.

In feudal Japan, women are less important than their counterparts. There were hardly any women in high places in the social orders, and the right to freedom was low. The women of upper classes typically had no say in choosing whom they marry, and their families decided the marriages.

All classes of women had the same thing in common. They had no freedom to re-marry once they were widowed, but men could re-marry anytime. Women could not get divorced, and due to this reasoning, many women committed suicide to escape from an unhappy or abusive union.

The low-ranking women had more freedom than the higher classes, and the low-ranking women did not go into unwanted marriages. The upper-class married to go to a higher social level.

The role of lower-ranking women was to serve their husbands before serving their fathers before marriage. Their duties included: serving their families, looking after their children, looking after animals and crops, cooking for their families, cleaning, and carrying out the household duties. A wife of a tradesman helped in their family business and other varied tasks.

Some of the women decided to become nuns, and women took part in more religious events than men. The writing of poetry was essential to upper-class women, and many become poets.

The close-knit families of the characters of this novel suffered tragedies through the death of loved ones. Happiness peeked around the corner with new births and new expectations.

When the Nightingale Sings

The circle of life remains unbroken as the family line continues. The next generation will reign with confidence and love. The samurai will rule until it rules no longer. Time changes and life untangles. "When the nightingale sings,"—it will bring a breath of serenity and protection.

Made in the USA
Middletown, DE
18 September 2023

38624924R00220